When My Wings Are Done

Robert E Lafond

Inquiries and Book Orders should be addressed to:

Great Writers Media
Email: info@greatwritersmedia.com
Phone: 877-600-5469

ISBN: 978-1-960605-16-0 (sc)
ISBN: 978-1-960605-18-4 (hc)
ISBN: 978-1-960605-17-7 (ebk)

INTRODUCTION

Angels? Wings? Do they exist? Many people think so, and it's not just the reverent of the different religions that believe. For many, angels are the afterlife leftovers of a past they no longer belong to. Heaven is a place mentioned in conversation with children or the afore-mentioned reverent, a place filled with visages of loved ones wearing wings; they fly about in all their glory, filled with happiness. But do those same believers aspire to the idea some angels might positively interfere in their lives?

The RULES in Heaven are sacrosanct. Angels cannot break those rules. They are not allowed to interfere in the lives of the people on earth. They can't call or write letters to their loved ones. They are supposed to do those things before we leave this earth.

One soul had a difficult time leaving. Horrifically interrupted in her living she had to do what she could to see someone left behind was going to be alright. She broke the rules by refusing to accept her wings until she was ready.

Sometimes an angel will act very subtly, offering whispers and suggestions of what you should do; that 'fly in your ear,' so to speak. But love can be disguised, and for Olivia, Harry and Ellie, it's a push in the pool."

CONTENTS

Any similarity between individuals living or deceased is purely coincidental. Any similarities between geographical locations actual or fictional is purely coincidental and inferences made are not intended to besmirch, malign, or otherwise harm the reputation of that location or the people residing there-in.

When My Wings Are Done is purely a work of fiction, solely and entirely the work of the author. Any attempt to add or subtract, copy or duplicate, malign or misinterpret passages from the original work, without first securing written permission from the author or his legal representative, will be met with litigation.

REL

CAST OF CHARACTERS

Angels	George & Alexander
Guardian Angel	Harry
Father	Donald Ackworth
Mother	Liz Johnson
Son	Harry Ackworth
1st Pilot	Lt. Col. James Perry
Flight Engineer	Chuck Gamer
Wife	Veronica Johnson
Daughter	Olivia Gamer
Comm. Embry-Riddle	Maj. Gen. Harold Reynolds
2nd Pilot	Capt. Charles Howe
3rd Pilot	Wm. Regents
Therapist	Elouise Haines
Harry's son	Wm. Ackworth
Daughter	Virginia Ackworth
Grandfather	Oliver Ackworth
Wife	Alice Johnson
Mechanic (1950)	Lt. Sam Johnson
Wife	Olivia Hancock
Commander Barksdale Air base	Maj. Gen. George Hancock

CHAPTER 1

Angels, George & Alexander

"George? Oh, George," Alexander calls George to discuss what he sees below.

"What is it, Alex?" he asked.

"Look!" Alexander pointed to a little house in Rhode Island, where a young couple was about to give birth to their first child.

"Oh, boy," George said in resignation. "Another one from that neighborhood. Is it a boy or a girl?"

"Don't know yet," Alex told him.

"I'll take a trip up to see the Boss," George said.

"But the Boss already knows, right?" Alex asked.

"Yes," George groans. "…and that means the colors have already been chosen, and a life plan. I really don't like it when the Boss does that."

"You don't have to worry about it, George, we only work in production," Alex reminds him.

"But these people go in and out of their scheduled plan, forcing us to change the color and the shape of the wings…by the time we're done the wings become unrecognizable. And he, or she, must accept them."

"Yeah, it's a little aggravating, I know, George. The Boss makes us wait, sometimes, extending the persons time down there with a little more life, a little more strength. And why? Because He feels they are not ready. I don't get it either, George, but it's not our job to worry."

"Well, I seem to recall when the end came when we were in battle, we had to take what we were given when we got here. There was no choice. And when you come up here with a lot of guys, man-ufacturing only has time to make white. Nothing fancy. You got a white set, Alex?"

"Yeah, and I had to wait in line with 5000 other guys. Those Peloponnesian wars were hell." Alex realized what he had said,

"OOPS! Sorry, Boss. That just slipped out."

"Don't worry about it, Alex. Those wars were hell," George told him.

"I never did ask you, George, why you have that red and blue swish on your wings."

Revolutionary War, Alex. I'm younger than you. I was carrying our flag when we got to the Delaware River, but I never got to carry it across. A musket ball hit me in the chest, and it was all over. I'm glad it ended quickly. I did not want to be standing in line with all the other guys waiting for my wings. I was handed these and I felt special. They fit well, and the colors are outstanding. The Boss gave me the job of watching over production. I feel more important here, now, than I ever did down there."

"Why didn't you feel important down there, George?"

"It's a long story, Alex. You don't want to hear it, again. You may have even seen it unfold."

"True, I may have, but good movies are better the second time around. And I think we've got time enough on our hands for you to tell it," Alex explained.

"Funny, Alex…time on our hands. Alright, find a comfy cloud and I'll tell you…"

I was born on a farm in Philadelphia, Pennsylvania. It was 1760, and my father managed fifty acres of vegetables and fruit trees, and several hundred acres of grassland for the scores of cattle he fed. Before I turned 10, I was in the barn milking cows and shoveling out the leftovers. My father taught me how to plant the crops for a successful harvest. The only thing I couldn't do was throw the eighty-pound bales of hay. I would have to grow a bit more before accompanying my brothers in harvesting the fields.

I was the smallest of my father's six sons, not getting any taller than five feet, I was spared most of the heavy work around the farm. And my father despised me because of my height. He couldn't scorn my abilities, though. I beat my brothers in everything, especially hunting. I would bring back the biggest buck, the tallest moose, the fattest bear. I could throw an ax farther and hit more targets dead center than my father.

Then the war came to the farm, and I had to stand by and watch my father knuckle under to the cruelty of the British troops ravaging the farm for food. I swore I would never give in to them. I told my father I was going to join General George Washington's Army on the Potomac.

He told me I was too short, that a musket was fully longer than I was tall. I pressed him saying,

"I'll get a job. I will convince the General I want to serve. I'll argue with all the sergeants, captains, and colonels about letting me serve." I made my petition to General Washington. He wrote back saying,

"Any man willing to risk his life for God and country, can serve in my army." The General's aide discounted my height and made me flag bearer. I carried the battalion's colors through three campaigns.

It wasn't until we got to the Delaware when it all hit the fan. Carrying that banner nice and high, and she was waving so beautifully, I shouldn't have paused as long as I did, to admire it. Somebody had the time to draw a bead on me, and they did not miss. That little round ball ripped into me and came out the other side. I went down gazing at my flag, closed my eyes and woke up here.

"Why the blue and the red on your wings, George?"

"They are for the blue and the red on the flag. It kind of looks like the flag I carried, doesn't it?"

"Yeah, somewhat. But what about this new guy down there? What is he going to amount to? What color wings will we be building for him?"

"I don't know, Alex. The Boss gives them free will, but you know, He's pulling strings when He wants to. Where that baby goes and what he does, we'll know in the end what color and what shape we make for him."

"Do you know who is going to watch him, George? Who his Guardian Angel is?"

"The last time I checked, Harry was up."

"You've got to be kidding me. That old guy hasn't had a set of whites awarded since the Philistine Wars and the Boss had to get in on that one. The people of Israel almost came home that day, George. There would have been a great many wings given out."

"Hey, the Boss knows what he's doing. Roster or no, Harry's got the call. We can check up on him from time to time and find out how he's doing, but he's not going to tell much. Harry likes to keep all his clients hush-hush until they get here. Just sit back and watch, see what happens. We've got time."

CHAPTER 2

Harry on Harry

Rhode Island was experiencing its worst winter storm in recorded history. It was February 1978, and Donald and Elizabeth Ackworth are stuck in their home. They need to get out and get Elizabeth to the hospital to have her baby. She was lying on blankets, on the floor, in front of the fireplace.

The house was old but strong. Donald had extra insulation put in last Fall after hearing projections for the coming Winter. But this storm was especially brutal. The winds were tearing at the shingles on the rooves of the houses around the neighbor-hood and constantly beating against the house. He had brought in enough wood for a full day and the cellar was loaded for the remainder of winter.

Don checked the amount of snow that had built up against the house. It was almost four feet high on the level ground, and the drifts against the side by the garage were close to the roof line. Reinforcing the roof last fall was a good idea even if it was a little expensive. He hoped the phone lines would be back up and operating again, having gone down with the power lines during the night. There was no electricity and nothing in the house was working unless it was on batteries. No stove for cooking, no television for news about the storm, no lights, other than from the fireplace and a few hurricane lamps spread throughout the house. And a baby was about to be born.

Elizabeth looked at her husband and asked, "Can we do this by ourselves, Don? Can you help me bring our baby into the world?"

"I don't know, hon. You know more about this than I do."

"We both brought it on, sweetheart. We both should have something to do about getting it born. OOH!" she grimaced.

"Don't do that, Liz," Don asked her.

"It hurts, hon. What do you want me to do, whistle Dixie?"

"Only if it helps with the pain," he said.

"Why don't you get a pot, fill it with water and place it by the fireplace. We might be able to get it to boil." Liz told him.

"What do you want to do, make soup?" he asked.

Liz started to laugh and told him it was something everybody does when a woman is going to have a baby.

"I saw it on TV, Dr. Kildare, or something."

Don brought out a stock pot filled with water and placed it on the hearth in front of the fire. He then brought out three or four towels, and an extra pillow for Liz, when she was ready to have the baby. He looked at his wife and said, "I think I saw the same show."

Suddenly there was a knock on the door. They looked at each other, wondering…

"Who in God's name is out in this stuff?" Donald asked.

"I can't imagine," Liz said. "Go and see, Don. Someone might be in trouble."

Don opened the door and saw an elderly, heavy-set woman standing there. He thought she looked familiar, so he let her in.

"My word, woman. What are you doing out there in this storm? How did you ever get around? How could you make it to the front door?" he asked her.

"Determination," she said in a thick French accent. "And you ask too many questions."

"I remember, your wife is pregnant. She doesn't have much time before the child will be born, yes? I came to help in case the baby, he comes tonight."

Liz looked up and told her, "It wasn't my choice to have it tonight, but thank you for thinking of us."

"Oh, that's alright. I do this all the time," the woman said. It was Harry, the old Guardian Angel. His assignment was the newborn. He was standing outside, waiting for Elizabeth to go into labor before he knocked on the door. Disguises come in handy when an angel is assigned someone. He whispered in Donald's ear, "I like the name Harry. What do you think?"

Donald looked up and wondered where that fly came from. He shooed it away.

"I'll wait to see what the baby looks like," he thought.

The French woman, Harry, told Liz, "When you think you are ready, blow very hard, and push at the same time. Don't stop unless I tell you to stop." Watching Liz's face the woman said,

"Push, hard, push," the old woman told Liz. "And blow, keep blowing. I have the head, don't stop. Here comes the shoulders and one arm, now the other arm. Here come the boy's legs and feet, and he is out. You are all done, madame." Harry told her.

Liz gave a resounding, "Yes," and smiled as the French woman cleaned up the child, who brought out an ear-piercing scream and the obligatory cry. Then she placed the baby on Liz's chest. "Your child has very good lungs, congratulations, madame, monsieur."

"Donald, look. Look at your son." Donald took the boy from Liz and held him up to thank God then held him to his chest. The boy snuggled down and never made a sound. Liz asked,

"What name do you want for him, Don?"

"You know, I've thought about it, over and over and the one name that keeps coming back is Harry, not Harold, or Hap or any other derivative, but Harry...Harry Ackworth, and he is my son."

Liz smiled to see the happiness on her husband's face.

"Then, Harry Ackworth it is. I like the name, too. Now I'm tired. I want to sleep. Are you going to hold him for a while, hon?"

"Yes. You sleep. When he wakes and gets hungry, I'll give him back to you."

Liz slept almost two hours while Don walked around the house with his son in his arms. He talked to Harry and told him,

"Harry, you will be an independent person, always have a choice. Your mother and I will teach you how to think first and act second. And I will never leave you until my wings are ready."

The old French woman looked at Elizabeth sleeping, then looked at Don cradling his son. She smiled to hear him speak of his wings. Sometime in the peace and joy of that evening, the woman, angel Harry, slipped out the door. The storm had ceased it ferocity and the power and telephone returned to service. Don looked around the room to thank the old woman only to find she had gone. He opened the door to find her but only found three feet of snow had drifted against the door. There were no tracks or any sign of anyone having come to the house.

He gave little Harry to Elizabeth when he noticed three men coming toward the house carrying bags.

"What on earth could these men possibly want on a morning like this?" he thought.

"Good morning," the first of the three men greeted Don.

"I'm from the St. Vincent DePaul Society and these brave souls are from the Salvation Army. They've come to help me distribute food and supplies to those folks who are most in need."

"Well, come in, get out of the weather. My wife and I just had a baby." Don told them.

"You delivered the child all by yourself?" one man asked.

"No. An old French woman came by in the heart of the storm and helped my wife with the delivery. She was a God-send." Don explained.

"We've been out all night helping the National Guard find people in trouble and we've seen no one, especially and old woman, walking these streets. No one is out, and you say she knocked on your door."

"Yes. She said she knew Elizabeth was pregnant and came by thinking the baby might come tonight. We were lucky she was here."

The three men smiled at one another and nodded their heads in agreement. "Please accept these supplies. We think you will need them. Keep that fire going. The power is sporadic, at best, though the phone lines are up. God bless you and stay warm. You have a special baby there. Good day."

As the three men left and Don was closing the door, he heard them say, simultaneously,

"God-Send!"

CHAPTER 3

1st Change

The winter snows melted away as the months passed, and Little Harry Ackworth grew quickly. From his 6lb. 10oz. beginning, he was putting on almost a pound a month and adding inches to his height. By the time the crocuses were popping their heads up, Harry had grown to near 21 inches and close to 11 lbs.

He never shied away from showing off his baby smile whenever Don and Liz would show him off to their family and friends. It was almost as if he had personal control, a turn on-turn off kind of. Don noticed and told the boy,

"You keep that up all your life and you will have women begging to be your wife."

Liz looked at Don and said,

"Don't say that, Donald. That could get the boy in big trouble."

"Yes, I know. I'm just warning him now."

"Oh, a lot of good that will do him," she said. "All we can do is let him grow up experiencing the opposite sex as he may or may not know how to. If he needs help, I 'm sure he'll ask you." Liz laughed, wondering what a son would ask his father.

Harry got to know the other children born in the neighborhood during the storm. The parents of them all were calling the group the 'Storm Kids', as if they were a club. One parent went so far as to have shirts made with Storm Kids printed on the back. All the children were born within one hour of one another. When birthdays came, they celebrated the seven children together.

Don and Elizabeth wanted to make sure their son grew up as an All-American boy and not sissified as some boys become because they have no brothers or sisters. But there were three girls in the Storm Kids, so Harry had his family of brothers and sisters growing up. Don enrolled Harry in junior Babe Ruth baseball. The boy played like a natural, surprising his parents. He excelled in any position he was played and often hit homeruns. As he advanced to higher and higher leagues, by high school Harry Ackworth became the one player in the league no one wanted to go up against.

At 18, while getting ready for his senior year, Harry's father was killed in an auto accident coming home from work. Don was Harry's mentor, having taught his son all things good and honest in the world. The one true advocate in everything Harry ever did, was now gone. But Don talked to Harry about death and what it means. How we can't control it and that "everybody gets a turn," his dad would joke. None the less, the pain of losing someone he loved was very real and hurt for a time.

Harry remembered many of the things his father had told him. Reading a letter his father wrote…

"Harry, you have to learn to put my life and my death in perspective. What I did, what I didn't do will matter now as examples to you. Who I loved and who I scoffed? Did I treat you and your mother with all the love I had to give? If you come up with a positive answer all the time, then I guess my wings were ready and it was time for me to go."

Harry teared up reading the letter his father had left behind for him, 'For My Son…To be opened upon my death,' was on the envelope. A second letter was left for Liz, who wept as she read it. She turned to her son and said,

"We must honor your father's wishes now. As he did for us, we must now do for him, and celebrate his life and all he accomplished."

The funeral for Donald Ackworth was a simple gathering of family and friends in the tiny church they attended. There was no mass, as Don wanted, just a simple send off with a blessing and a little sprinkling of Holy Water. The reception afterward was quite the opposite. Family and friends filled the hall enjoying the food and the beer and Don's favorite music.

But in his letter, Don insisted the gang listen to a few Barbershop songs. He was a member of the local chorus for almost 15 years and insisted a least a quartet sing at the memorial. The *Clefs of Danger* sang for more than an hour to a rousing applause. The leader of the quartet, and one of Don's best friends, saluted his friend with the Irish Blessing.

Harry and his mother were pleased at the number of friends that attended the wake, the funeral, and the memorial. The funeral home was very helpful in arranging the order of everything. Liz was too heartbroken to take care of it. Harry didn't know whether to turn left or right at times, now that his father was gone.

In the late evening hours as mother and son would try to figure out what they would do now, without their leader they would fall asleep on the sofa, dreaming of the life they shared with Don. Harry, the Guardian Angel, would appear to the young man and speak to him in his dreams. His father would appear, and he and the Guardian Angel would be discussing young Harry's future. The boy would awaken suddenly, disturbed, and run to his mother.

"Mom, I saw dad again. This time he was with an angel and dad had wings. They were talking but I couldn't understand what about. I don't like these apparitions, mom. I don't understand them."

"I do, son. I've had the same dreams, sort of. Your father has come to me several times when I was crying, feeling very lonely, and missing him so much. He would tell me he was okay and that everything was going to be alright. He kept telling me our future would be a good one and not to worry. He said you and I had a Guardian Angel watching over each of us."

"Did dad say how to stop the pain? Is someone else supposed to come into our lives and make tomorrow easier for us? Dad and I discussed these things, mom, but never with the notion that someone was going to take his place." Harry had tears trying to explain the fear and the confusion.

"It'll be just you and me for a while, Harry. We must learn to get on by ourselves before we can let any other man enter our lives, and we have to build up our strength and succeed on our own. If your father is watching us, I think he would want it that way."

"That's fine by me, mom. I know you and I can do it. Dad taught us how. He told me during one of our talks that he would not be leaving until his wings were done. I didn't understand what that meant at the time, but after the dreams I've been having, I think I understand now. Dad always comes by with some goofy looking guy with wings looking all mussed up. I hope dad's wings don't look like that."

Harry and his mother laughed at the image he was telling her. "Son, I have had the same image of your father, but I haven't seen the goofy looking one."

"Go to bed, son. If your father shows up again, just welcome him and listen. He must surely have made connections to have earned his wings."

"Okay, mom." Harry went to bed, leaving is mother to sleep soundly on the sofa till morning.

CHAPTER 4

2nd Change

Harry had some good friends during his growing years, ever since the first grade. Billy Carpenter lived right across the street. He had a bike just like Harry's. The two would go riding together and spend so much time away from their houses their parents would have to go looking for them. Billy got a flat tire one day while they were riding along the railroad tracks.

"I guess you'll have to ride on the back of mine, Billy."

"I guess so, but I'm bigger than you, Harry. Can you peddle the both of us home?"

"I think so, Billy. We'll find out." The tracks abutted a road that didn't exactly lead in the direction of their homes. When they heard the train coming, they got on the road and started heading in the direction they thought was the way home. It was lot easier to peddle, but Harry tuckered out after a while. Billy took his turn peddling and Harry rode on the back.

Darkness seemed to come quickly, and they were afraid they were lost. It was now well past their supper hour, and both sets of parents set out in great worry to find where their sons had gone. Don had heard the train go by and immediately thought of looking down the tracks. Billy's father went with him while their mothers went in the opposite direction. After walking two miles, they found Billy's bicycle with a flat tire.

"That means they're riding together. Harry knows enough to know which way is home, so I think they headed back. And that road would have made it easier for them to peddle. With dark setting in, those boys are going to be scared. That road veers away from the direction of our homes. Let's head that way. I think we can make good time if we jog part way. We'll probably meet up with them."

The men had been out searching for almost an hour and the boys had been riding for more than three. Billy's dad spotted something moving in the road ahead of them and called out. The boys heard the call and stopped under a streetlamp to wait.

Don and Billy's dad saw the boys were ashamed of their behavior but also that they were scared. Both Harry and Billy ran up to their dads and gave them a big hug. Don looked at Harry and asked,

"Did you learn anything today, Harry, Billy?"

Billy spoke up and said, "Yeah, don't ride the railroad track with bad tires." His father laughed.

"And you son?"

"I learned I can't peddle Billy home like he can me. He's bigger and stronger than me."

The two men looked at one another and laughed at the boys.

"I'll get your bicycle tomorrow, Billy, and a new tire."

"Thanks dad."

"Is mom worried, dad?" Harry asked.

"Should she be, Harry?" his father asked.

"Yeah, I guess so. I'll apologize to her when we get home." Harry said.

"Good idea," his father added.

Harry and Billy went through grade school and high school together, competing for the highest grades in their classes. It was a 50/50 race all the way to graduation. Harry became Class President while Billy was Class Salutatorian.

Not long after graduation Harry got a letter from Billy's father. Billy was suffering from a rare form of Cancer and didn't have a lot of time left. He called for Harry. Harry rushed home from Embry-Riddle's Florida campus to be at Billy's side.

When he walked into Billy's hospital room Bill's mother and father looked at Harry and stepped aside so the two could be alone together.

"Bill?" Harry called.

Bill looked at his friend of so many years and tears began to fall. Harry fought so hard not to cry, wanting to be strong, but broke down. He asked his friend,

"Billy, why didn't you tell me you were sick? Why did I have to hear from your father and so late?"

"There's nothing you could have done, my friend. This Cancer didn't creep up on me. It came and it dug in, and no matter what the doctors tried, nothing worked. I didn't want you coming out of school to see me like a guinea pig, and that's what I was this past year."

"But your letters said nothing, Billy."

"I couldn't tell you, Harry. I just couldn't tell you. But I'm glad you're here. I get to see you one last time, and I remember what your dad said, about…going. That he wasn't going until his wings were done. I guess my wings must be done, Harry."

"You've been my best friend for all these years. I couldn't ask for one better. Always remember me, will ya, Harry?"

Harry grabbed Billy's hand and the two held onto one another until Harry felt Billy's hand loosen and finally go limp.

"Billy?" he called, and when Billy didn't respond and his monitor sounded, Harry got up, and as they did every time, they parted saying, 'See you later Storm Kid'. He waved goodbye to his childhood friend and walked out to the hallway to meet his mother. There he saw Billy's mom while his dad was in with Billy and the doctors.

Bill's dad came out and hugged his wife then walked over to Harry and gave him a big tear-filled hug.

"Billy didn't want me to tell you, Harry. He made me promise, and it was hard for me to keep that promise, but I did it for Bill. The two of you have been the best of friends for so very long, I could not imagine friends being any closer than you two. Don't forget him, Harry, and don't forget us. If you ever need anything, just ask. We owe that to Billy."

"Thank you, Mr. Carpenter, Mrs. Carpenter. The only thing I would ask is that you watch my mother while I'm away. Continue to be her friend as you have always been, and I will be forever grateful."

"We can do that, Harry. Your dad was my best friend, and I miss him, but we can do that."

CHAPTER 5

A Friendly Turn

Harry went back to Embry-Riddle Aeronautical University to complete his studies in Aeronautical Engineering. Daytona Beach was a fun place for Harry to attend college, but after four years on the beach and flying over the ocean, Harry made a change and extended his education at the University campus in Prescott, Arizona. Between entrances Harry went home to be with his mother. He met a new man in her life and found something familiar in their conversations. He was a former Air Force pilot and flew the aging B-52 bomber.

Harry asked him, "How does it feel, now that you're retired, telling people you piloted a war horse like the B-52?"

Ret. Colonel James Perry looked at Harry with nothing but pride and told him, "Glorious. Prideful. Very Special."

"That is one ride I would like to take." Harry told him.

"I can do that for you, son, especially since you're enrolled with Embry-Riddle and have taken all their flying courses. I still have a few debts owed me I think I can collect on."

Harry was glad he had come home to see his mother but wondered of this new man in her life. A handsome face, a strong build, and a kind demeaner might be enough to fill the place his father occupied.

Jim Perry placed a phone call to a friend living in Barksdale, Louisiana. Chuck Gamer was Jim's navigator when they rode the B-52s together several years ago. Chuck stayed in Louisiana for the Cajun food and the roar of the -52's every time they took off. He answered the phone,

"Hello, Chuck here."

"Aren't you ever going to change that answering machine?" Jim asked.

Chuck knew who was calling, "Well, Sir, if I knew I was going to get a call from my pilot, I would have let the machine take the call. How are you doing, Colonel?"

"I'm good Chuck, and you?"

"Doing all right, sir. I am not about to complain. My wife's got some jambalaya on the stove, and we are going to eat good tonight. Why don't you come by for a bite? We can sit and talk a while, have a brew-ski, and dream of dancing among the clouds at thirty-thousand."

"I would so much like that Chuck, but right now I'm in Rhode Island visiting my lady friend."

"Oh, That's too bad. Anyway, what's on your mind, Jim?"

"Is there the possibility of getting a ride on a 52 the next time they have a check flight?"

"Wow. That's quite a request. Are you lonesome for left seat, Jim? Feeling like you need a fix?" Chuck laughed.

"Actually, I could use a fix in the left seat, but I've also got a young man that needs a push into Air Force Aeronautics. He's been through Embry, got his Bachelor's. He is quite knowledgeable in aviation practices, the field of aeronautics and has his private license. He took courses in commercial and is certified to take passengers. He's got his instrument rating and is night capable. In the fall he's going back to Embry in Prescott to work on his Masters. He's the guy I want to take up. We can always sit in the bomb-bay. If they don't like us, they can open the doors. Do you think you can get us a ride?"

"Let me find out. I want to say you may have to move on a moment's notice. How long would it take you to get here from that tiny state?"

"We can be there in 12hours flight time. We might have to stay overnight one day. Would that hold things up?"

A short pause followed, and Chuck returned with,

"Stay glued to the phone, colonel. We can catch up when you get here."

"Good enough, Chuck. Thanks a lot. I'll wait for your call." Jim closed the conversation smiling at the thought of the look on Harry's face when he tells him.

Jim went back to an apartment he was renting at a B&B along the Rhode Island coast. The difference in scenery, atmosphere, even the air, awakened his senses every morning. After 35 years in the Air Force, base after base, feeling grounded and purposeful felt good. His life was beginning to root again and he was enjoying the company of Elizabeth Ackworth, Harry's mother.

Anxious to call Harry and share the news he thought,

"What am I going to tell him? I have to wait for Chuck's phone call." He wanted to make a good impression on Harry, figuring if he did that, their relationship would have a better footing. Chuck called back in two hours.

"Jim, bad news. I cannot get you a ride, not even on a ferry. The ships are on standby 24/7, and maintenance is the same. The B-52 has to be ready at the drop of a hat. The best I can do is get permission for him to get on base. He can have a walk around and maybe get a peek into the cockpit. Fill the boy in with what you know, colonel. You and I flew the Beast for 10 years, and I'm the only guy that remembers you from those days."

Jim paused before answering.

"That is disappointing, Chuck, but I understand the need for security is still there. I figured the easy times today would make it easier for him to get a ride."

"Well, why don't you come on down anyway, colonel. Bring the boy and his mother. I've got plenty of room here at my place. Veronica and I don't get a lot of company. We could use the chance to entertain, especially and old friend and the chance to make a new one. Talk it over with him, then let me know. If I don't hear from you in a few days, I'll know you can't make it."

"Sounds good, Chuck. I'll see the boy and his mother today. I'll give you a call after discussing it with them. Thanks for trying, Chuck."

"Shit! That was disappointing. Well, I'll drive up and tell him. I want to see Liz anyway."

The rented convertible was the perfect vehicle today. The open-air driving was all Jim rented no matter where he was stationed. Even the dead-cold of the Minot winters brought the occasional sunny drop-the-top days. The natives thought he was crazy and better heads did prevail as the tolerance level went down. But stationed on southern bases around the world had Jim searching for the convertible to rent.

He pulled into Liz's driveway and could see her and Harry sitting by the pool in the back yard. He waved as he went around back carrying a six pack and some fried sea food.

"Harry, Liz, I brought lunch."

She got up to greet him and asked, "What did you do this time?"

"You are going to go broke if you don't stop buying things every time you come over. Harry and I were just discussing your last visit."

"Anything I can add to the conversation?" Jim asked.

"Well, yes, there is. I'll have Harry get it started," Liz said.

"Hello, Harry, how are you?"

"I am well, sir, and yourself?"

"Well, I came bearing gifts because my news is not all good news, I'm afraid. I can't get you that ride on a 52. It seems security has closed up any chance of getting one. The ships have to be ready at all times. You know, on standby, and nothing can get in their way. My friend in Louisiana said you might get permission to walk around, even get a look inside the cockpit, but it would be a very quick look-see. We've been invited down to his place to spend a little time, have a mini-vacation you might say. Do you have some time before you go back to school?"

"I do, and I would love to visit your friend and see Louisiana. I would be happy just to walk around and see the Beast, touch its wrinkled skin, maybe."

"There are always new possibilities waiting, Harry."

Jim looked at Liz, waiting for a positive sign from her that Chuck's plan was a go. She could see the two men in her life were excited about it and wanted it to happen. She asked,

"Alright. How do we get down there? Drive? Fly? And when do we leave? Wait, I must go shopping. I don't have anything to wear."

"Mom, you've got plenty of things to wear."

"Why do women have to go shopping when they're not going anywhere special? It's Louisiana, Liz. It might be a little warm down there so you should wear light clothing, but certainly nothing special."

"I just don't want your friend seeing us in a bad light. He might think we're just, 'Northerners!'" she exclaimed.

"Liz, Chuck is from Minnesota. He chose to live in Louisiana because the B-52s are there. If the government ever decided to close that base or move the Wing to a new base, Chuck would follow. He has spent more time with the Beast than I did. He knows that plane better than anybody I know. Think we're 'Northerners?' Yeah, and he would welcome it. You don't have to worry about that, hon."

That word, Hon! It struck an odd feeling in Harry. Before now, he didn't quite know how to handle this new man in his mother's life. Jim wasn't really in his life because he was away at school most of the year. But hearing that word, Hon! How does he take that?"

"With resignation, I guess. Mom is entitled to a man-friend. Dad's been gone almost 5 years now," Harry thought to himself.

"I can hardly believe it, and I miss you, dad. But it looks like mom's going to move on and you know it's time. It looks like he's a good man, dad. Mom seems happy. I don't know how long they've been seeing one another. You know more than I do so you must think it's all okay. I can go along with that, dad, so long as mom is happy."

Jim spoke up, "Do you know when you would like to leave, Harry?"

"I'm good anytime, but I'll wait for mom. Most of my stuff is still in my suitcase. I'll grab enough for a backpack, and I'll be all set. Are you set, Jim?"

"I'll head back to my room, and call my friend, tell him we're flying down. I can pack some things for a few days and be right back here. See you in an hour."

Jim left to go back to his B&B. He called Chuck to say he would be flying down in the Lockheed and to meet him at the airport.

"If things go on time, Chuck, I'll see you around 2000hrs."

"Good enough," Chuck told him. "I'll be there."

Harry wasn't yet told that Jim owned a twin engine plane, but Jim hadn't told Liz either. He was waiting for the right time to spring all that on his new 'family.' He held hopes they would be his new family and he was working hard that everything would go well.

He got back to the house and found Liz and Harry were ready to go.

"Oh," he commented. "You did have things to wear, and you packed light, good." He looked at Harry and emphasized,

"You can't overload an aircraft, can you, Harry?"

"Well, you shouldn't, but it is easy to make that mistake. But Jim, we have a weight limit on commercial flights. I don't think we're going to make that limit combined."

"I didn't tell you before because I wanted to keep it a surprise until the right time…and I guess this is the right time."

"What is it, Jim? Do you own a plane? Are you borrowing a plane? Which is it?" Harry pressed.

"Let's get loaded up and on the road. You'll see when we get to the airport. I've called ahead and had a crew get my plane ready. You'll like it, Harry. I promise you will."

CHAPTER 6

Getting To Know You

Jim parked the convertible in the well-lit and maintained, Long-Stay lot. The car would sit under an overhang, but the forecast was good for the following week. The three went into the terminal and found their way down through a maze of hallways to a hangar. Harry walked out into the hangar and dropped his bag. In front of him sat a Lockheed 12A Electra Junior. She was polished aluminum with a thin black stripe running the length of the fuselage. Twin rotary engines sat one on each wing. She was a tail dragger of the most beautiful type.

"I purchased her from a guy in Arizona several years ago," Jim said. "He bought an original Piper Cub Cadet from a guy in Seekonk, Mass. That guy was selling the Cub because his wife did not want him flying anymore. The three of us got together that first night and swapped paperwork, checks, and great stories over a fantastic meal and fine drinks. After all the legal work was done, I parked her here and began working on her to bring her up to modern day. The most expensive part of the renovation was the radio work. It's all digital now and I get up-dates every six months of the latest maps and regulations. I can fly anywhere in the world and be up to date."

Harry walked around touching the shiny surface and inspecting the ailerons and rudder. He looked inside the engine cowlings and marveled at the cleanliness of the engines.

"May I board her, Jim?"

"You certainly may, Harry. As a matter of fact, we should all board so we can make Louisiana in good time. It's 1500 miles, and though a commercial jet is faster, it is not as much fun. And I will keep the air-pockets and bumps down to a manageable level. I think you will enjoy the ride, and the more you enjoy it the shorter the trip will be."

Ginny's Gin was rolled out of the hangar onto the tarmac. Jim got into the left seat and Harry was given the privilege of the right seat. Liz took a comfortable seat in the cabin and smiled in her heart at the interaction between her son and her new beau. Harry was thrilled to be sitting in the cockpit of such a classic plane.

"Your mom tells me you've got stick time from lessons in school. Nothing as large as this though, am I right?"

"Nothing as large, or as beautiful, as this," Harry said, trying to take in all the up-to-date avionics.

"It seems a little odd to be sitting in such a modern cockpit of an antique airplane; two rotary engines, a twin boom tail section. It's like going through some sort of mixed-up time-warp."

Jim laughed at Harry's assessment. "I know, I felt something like that after I had the instruments installed. Every-thing worked the way it should, but after all my years in the Air Force, in and out of different types, especially the B-52, and hearing the roar of the radials, I truly expected gauges in front of me. But I've moved into the 21st century and I know how to read and operate these instruments."

"Are you ready to fly?" he asked Harry.

Harry responded excitedly, "Hell, yes."

Then Jim asked Liz, "Are you ready, sweetheart?"

"Take her up!" she said.

Jim flipped the igniter and the right engine cranked over with the grunt of a weightlifter with too much weight. He waited for the rpms to come up and turned the left engine over. Harry watched and listened as the right engine smoothed out, and the vibrations settled down. The left engine soon followed, and Jim radioed the tower for taxi instructions.

"It might seem a little bumpy now, that's just the runway. It'll be a much smoother ride once we're off the ground." He turned in his seat to see Liz looking out the window. "How are you doing back there?"

"I'm doing fine. When will the flight attendant be around?"

Jim laughed and told her, "There are drinks and sandwiches in the cooler in front of you. You can get up once we're airborne." The he went into his commercial voice,

"Passengers will observe the no smoking/seat belt sign until we have reached our service altitude. We will be flying today at an altitude of 15,000 feet and should reach our destination in 6hours, 45 minutes with one refueling stop in Raleigh/Durham. You will find the call button above your head should you want anything. The flight attendant will be glad to help you. Sit back and enjoy the flight."

Harry never heard Jim on the intercom. He was too busy studying the instrument panel. He took a break in his dreaming to ask Jim, "Why did you call her *Ginny's Gin?*"

"I don't think they taught you this in school, but airplanes have always had female names. Many of the bombers during WWII had women's names or inferences to women. A B-29 had 'Necessary Evil 'with a voluptuous blonde alongside, and the 'Enola Gay, another B-29,' which dropped the bomb on Hiroshima. My father had pictures of 'Poison Ivy' and the 'Memphis Belle.' They all had pin-up girls being referred to. So, I wanted something a little different and came up with *Ginny's Gin.*"

"I remember hearing something about the names but never knew why they were chosen."

Jim whispered, "It's because women have a cock pit, and a plane has a cock pit." He gazed at Harry adding, "Get it?"

"I got it," Harry laughed. "Fitting."

"We are at 12,000ft. Take the wheel, will ya, Harry? I'm going back to check on your mom."

"Wait! Wait, Jim. I've never flown anything this big."

"What's the biggest you've managed?" Jim asked.

"A 190 (Cessna 190)."

"Well," Jim paused. "Pretend this is a 190 with two engines. Keep her steady and you'll be fine. I'll be back in a minute."

Harry grabbed the wheel and all at once felt the twin Pratt & Whitney radials humming through the fuselage. The air was clear, the ride was smooth, for the most part. An occasional up draft or down draft would cause the plane to veer a little and Harry would have to correct.

Jim went back to the cabin to check on Liz and found her asleep. He covered her with a blanket, kissed her forehead, and went back to the cockpit. "How does she feel, Harry?"

"Amazing," Harry told him and gave the wheel back to Jim.

"No, Harry. You keep the wheel. You've got it. If you run into trouble I'm right here. Your mother is sleeping and that says a lot about her confidence in my flying. I would rather she was sleeping than feeling nervous all over the place."

"You're right. Mom does get nervous about new things. I don't think she and my dad did any flying…but that seemed so long ago," Harry dreamed.

Jim caught the reference of Harry's father and he, too, fell back, for a moment, into the memory of his first fiancé, Virginia Wales. They met when Jim was stationed in Southern California, about to be deployed to Afghanistan and the Bagram Air Base. Virginia was an Air Force brat; her father served in England during WWII.

Her tour of duty ended while Jim was in the air, and as he was landing the base came under attack. Rockets and mortars were missing the runway but not the quarters of the men and women staying there. Virginia was in one of those billets and died before she could get to a bunker. She and Jim were to be married when they both got back to the States. That was almost 30 years ago, and he never married. Girl friends came and went for lack of a serious relationship and for want of staying in the air.

After 10 years in the cockpit of a B-52, Jim retired from the Air Force as a full-bird colonel. He came to Rhode Island to visit his brother who had retired in Newport and was living on his Islander 36. The two stepped out to a night club one night and Jim bumped into Elizabeth who was out with one of her girlfriends. They spent the evening enjoying the music, conversation and an attraction they hadn't had in some time. That was a year ago.

Liz kept that liaison from Harry because she knew he would worry about his attractive mother going out in public to have a good time, meeting someone, and not knowing the good someone from the bad.

Right now, behind the wheel of Jim's plane, Harry was thinking Jim was the right guy for his mother, but he would not allow Jim to take his father's place. He felt too old for that kind of relationship again. Harry was on his own and growing while he was in school. His maturity also grew with every plane he took up and successfully brought back down.

They had been in the air for almost 4hours and it was time for Raleigh/Durham Airport to show up in the window.

"I'll take the wheel, Harry." Jim called the tower and was cleared to land. He used his intercom voice to tell Liz they were about to land and to be sure her seat belt was fastened. Jim pulled down a side apron in front of the main terminal. He traveled down to a hangar at the end of the runway was reserved for the *Ginny's Gin.* Art Bedford, the Hangar Man everybody called him, was there to meet the plane, get her in the hangar and do some minor maintenance so she would be ready for the trip home.

"Don't worry, Jim. I'll have *Ginny* ready when you need her."

Jim tossed Art the key as Chuck pulled up.

"Now," he exclaimed. "That is a fine pair of wings. You said she would be ready for a trip and by golly you got her done. How does she fly, Colonel?"

"I almost wish she had larger fuel tanks, and seats that were more inviting," he confessed as he rubbed his back side.

"Oh, yeah. I remember long trips we had to take as the war in Korea was beginning. Not comfortable at all. I wish so many times I had been chosen to make the Pacific crossing by boat. But that was long ago and far away. We'll leave that pone alone. Don't worry Jim, I'll have the *Gin* ready for you."

After a brief walk through the terminal to stretch their legs, they got back in the plane and laid their path to Baton Rouge, Louisiana, the last 800 miles. The remaining 500 miles of the trip were going to seem long after the first half of the trip. Since they hadn't bought anything to eat really, only the snacks, Harry went into the cooler and pulled out one of the sandwiches Jim had made yesterday morning.

"Oh, is this roast beef, Jim?" Harry asked.

"Yes, it is," Jim said. "Go ahead and take it if you like roast beef. That's hot mustard on the meat. It's quite good. Try it." Jim insisted.

"Hot mustard, huh?" Harry looked in wonder. "Well, I'll try half." He took half the sandwich and tasted it. "This would go very well with a nice beer, Jim."

"Yes, I know. That's how I usually enjoy my sandwiches when I'm watching a movie," Jim answered.

"Sorry. No beer, just good water," he added.

Liz asked, "What else did you plan on today, James?"

"I didn't forget you. sweetheart. Your peanut-butter and marsh-mallow is in there. Good luck getting it out of the baggy. The marsh-mallow is probably all over the place." Jim explained.

"That's alright," Liz added. "I am experienced in the art of digesting a Fluffer-Nutter, including licking the container holding the beautiful, white goo. Watch me. NO! Don't watch me. You keep your eyes on the road," Liz insisted, delicately trying to remove a dripping marshmallow and peanut-butter sandwich from the cooler. Harry handed her the carton of milk to enjoy down her white mess, while he took the Coke. Jim settled for the remaining half of the roast beef sandwich and the ginger ale. The drinks weren't very cold but did the job of washing clear their pallets.

Liz surprised the men in the plane by revealing a pack of cigarettes.

Jim said, "You, dear? Cigarettes?"

"Mom," Harry questioned. "When did you start smoking cigarettes?"

"I haven't started, or even considered, smoking, gentlemen. These are for you, two," Liz told them. She turned to Harry and handed him the lighter Ollie had bought him. I knew you would be needing this after a while."

"Geeze, thanks, mom." Liz handed Harry the pack. He opened it and offered the first one to Jim.

"Thanks, Harry. You'll find small ashtrays built into the walls. Just pulled down to open them."

Liz smiled as the two men in her life enjoyed their smokes. Fortunately, the smoke washed out the vents and did not bother her. She enjoyed watching them play with the smoke.

"Who knows how to make rings?" she asked

"Everybody knows how to make rings, dear," Jim said.

Harry made the first ring. As it floated toward the front, Jim blew one that intersected the first. Liz watched with a smile on her face as the rings melted away in the draft of the planes' ventilation. The two, 'boys,' played for an hour till the excitement died away. She saw some bonding beginning to take place.

"I hope the fun lasts between them. Harry only had his father for so long before he was taken…his wings were ready."

Everyone sat back to enjoy the ride and the view at 12500 ft. Next stop, Barksdale AFB, in Shreveport, Louisiana.

Jim got on the radio and called Chuck, telling him they would be landing in Shreveport in about 4hours. Chuck said he would be waiting for them.

"Well, Harry, what do you think of my plane?"

"It's wonderful. I never thought I could love flying this much. I'm not sure I want to ride in a B-52 now. The difference in planes would make an interesting study, but I would bet the difference in flying experience is enormous. You would know, Jim. You've experienced both."

"Yes, I have, and I much prefer the one I'm holding in my hands. I know the expense of owning and maintaining a plane like this, and I better understand the concern our government has on the budget the Air Force has to maintain our fleet of air defense. This is my escape, Harry. When you are finished school and you get into the career you want, perhaps you'll want to buy this baby."

"You want to sell, *Ginny?* "

"No, not now anyway. Maybe sometime down the road. We'll see."

C H A P T E R 7

Another Step

The *Ginny's Gin* made her approach to Barksdale with George Gamer watching from the terminal. As soon as the wheels touched down, he made his way to a hangar at the far end of the runway. The *Gin* pulled in front and George waited till the props stopped spinning. When the door opened Harry exited first to help his mother down the steps. Jim was right behind and stopped at the top of the steps. He spotted George, waiving, and smiling a big grin.

The two crew members of the *Winged One* exchanged man sized hugs and grins, patting each other on the back.

"How the hell are you, Colonel? How long has it been? Two, three years?" George asked.

"Check your calendar, George. I think you've lost a few years in between, but you've always been generous with your time. I'm doing good, and you?" Jim answered.

Patting his gut, "As you can see Colonel, being retired can have a detrimental effect on your waistline. Though it hasn't hurt you any! How was your flight?" ow was your flight?"

"Flight was long and in two hops, but I loved every minute. I have to take you up in it, George. You will love the radios," Jim added.

"She is a beauty, that's for sure. I would love a ride."

"Oh, George, this is Harry Ackworth, the young man I told you about, who wants to get a look see around the B-**52**."

"Nice to meet you, young man. It warms my heart to hear of young folks that want a career in aviation." Chuck said shaking Harry's hand.

"And this must be Elizabeth. Oh, I've heard so much about you, and I can see what Jim told me didn't do you justice. You are a pretty one."

"Well, thank you, Mr. Gamer. Please, call me Liz," she said, slightly embarrassed.

"You can drop that Mister stuff. Just call me Chuck and we will get along just fine. Did you folks bring along much luggage?"

"No," Jim told him, "Just overnight bags, Chuck. We are good for two or three days, if you can put up with us for that long."

"I have the rooms for you to stay as long as you like. Vicky and I welcome you with open arms. Now, let's get in the car and I'll give you a brief tour on the way to the house."

Chuck drove a restored 1955 Buick Roadmaster convertible. It was the same one he bragged of owning every day they sat aloft in flight. Jim stopped and looked at the car admiring the completion of Chuck's dream.

"The last thing I knew about this wreck was she was in the barn waiting for some tweaking. I see you did a lot more than that, Chuck. She is beautiful. Now, if she only had wings."

Liz and Harry smiled at the chance to ride in such a restored classic.

"Wow!" Harry exclaimed. "She is beautiful, almost as nice as the Electra. Like Jim said, 'If she only had wings.'"

"Oh, she can fly," Chuck said with admiration. "Maybe a little closer to the ground, but I don't have to call the tower for clearance. Get in, let's get going."

He gave them a sightseeing tour of the Louisiana countryside on the way to his place. South of the base across from the Red River National Wildlife Reserve, the river snakes it way down to Morgan City blending into the Atchafalaya River and a few smaller bayous. His place was only a hop, skip and a jump from anything in Shreveport, but the house sat at the far end of a development, the last house there. Chuck made sure no one else was going to build in that area by buying up the last few acres encircling his place. As they arrived, Jim made note of how handsome the house was.

"It's a beautiful home, Chuck. Did it take you long to build it?"

"Yeah, I guess. With the hurricanes we get down here, and weather advisories, they put things on hold sometimes, but, after 16 months, Veronica and I got it where we want, and though it seems big we don't feel crowded or squeezed into a matchbox like some of the other homes."

"And the pool kind of makes it even more livable by taking away any feeling of seclusion. I like my space and I figured this is enough to call mine without any interference. I get no kids down this end and I don't hear any traffic going by." Chuck explained.

"Just the roar of the 52s on take-off," I added.

"Yep, and a lovely sound it is." he insisted.

"Yes, it is, a bit loud, but heart-warming; air defense in action."

Veronica greeted them as Liz and Harry made their way into the house. "Welcome Elizabeth, Harry. Please make yourself at home. Can I get you a drink? You must be thirsty after such a long flight."

"I'll just have ice water, please," Liz said. "And call me Liz."

"And the same for me, thank you," Harry copied.

"This is a lovely home, Veronica," Liz commented.

"Oh, please, call me Vicky. And thank you. Chuck and I have spent quite a bit of time getting it where we want it, but I think we've finally made it. The pool was the last thing we did, and we have enjoyed it quite a bit. We have nice long summers. Did you bring swimsuits?" she asked.

"Oh, no. This trip was more for Harry and Jim. I came along for the ride and to see my son is happy in his chosen career. He wants more schooling and plans on continuing with Embry-Riddle in Prescott, Arizona. But I think Jim has whet Harry's appetite while flying in the Electra. It was an enjoyable flight, enough, so I was able to get some sleep. Harry truly enjoyed being upfront with Jim. The two hit it off rather well. I'm glad."

Harry didn't say a great deal. He was admiring the photos Chuck had around the living room. They were of the B-52 and several other great bombers the Air Force had in service in years past.

"These are great photos, Vicky." He told her, as Chuck and Jim were walking in from the pool.

"Oh, you like the pictures? Well, I've got a lot more to show you, and the stories to tell behind them."

"Not right now, dear. These people have had a long flight and I'm sure they are tired. It is getting late. They need their rest if you are planning a long day tomorrow. Come, Liz, I'll show you where you and Jim are staying."

Liz turned to look at Jim. She smiled crookedly as Jim smiled back, crookedly. This would be the first time her son would see another man sleeping with his mother. Harry smiled a broad grin and gave his mother approving eyes. "She is old enough," he thought.

"Harry, your room is down the hallway. The bathroom is right next door. When you're ready, goodnight."

Liz went to bed leaving Jim and Chuck to talk of the old days in the 52s. Harry left the men following his second beer.

"Enough is enough. Good night, gentlemen," he told them as he made his way to his bedroom.

"It looks like you and me, Colonel," Chuck said.

"Not for long, Sergeant. Retirement has made a stately old man of me. I need more sleep now than I ever thought I would need. But that's okay. I can still fill my days with what makes me happy."

"So, what are you doing besides working on the plane?"

"I've got a small design firm working on different projects, houses, furniture, landscaping. I even submitted a design for a small ultra-light aircraft you can build at home. The Air Force got hold of it and offered some ridiculous amount of money for everything I had on it. All I insisted was that my name stay on the original design. They could make any variant they wanted, and they did. But to no success. Now they are going back to the original design. I feel good about it. I succeeded again."

"That's great. When do I get to see your design in the air?"

"You may have already seen it, but it's mostly in the air at night. I designed it for fun, but the Air Force made it night- time surveillance, very quiet, stealthy. If you haven't seen it around here than it may not be here yet," Jim explained.

"What's it called; your design, I mean?" Chuck asked.

"I called it *Night Laughter*. The Air Force called it something strange, like Dark Joy or something, and gave it a numerical designation. The next time you go to the base ask about it. Somebody should be able to tell you something." Jim said.

"Well, we are going tomorrow. I finagled an appointment with the flight commander of the Wing stationed here. He's got one 52 in the shed and we have permission to get a look-see, but it'll be under guard. So, I don't know how much we will be allowed access to the bird."

"I think Harry will be happy with that. Say, maybe you could ask that wing commander about Dark Joy, or Night Laughter. He might know something."

"Good idea," Chuck remarked, "and with that dream in my head, I'll say goodnight. Liz is in the first bedroom on the left. Goodnight, Colonel."

"Goodnight, Chuck."

CHAPTER 8

Time Warp

About 1:00 AM the door to Harry's bedroom opened. A lone, slender figure crept in and attempted to crawl into bed unnoticed. Harry felt the person and immediately awakened to find a young lady, approximately his age, fully naked, and lying next to him.

"Who in hell are you, and why are you in my bed?" he whispered.

"This is my bed, and why are you sleeping in my bed?" she whispered in low tones, so as not to awaken the others in the house.

They both sat up and looked at one another, the young lady attempting to cover up.

"It's a little late for that now, don't you think?" Harry said.

"No." admonishing him. "What are you doing in my bed?"

"If this is your bed why did Victoria offer it to me for our stay here?"

"Offered it to you?" She attempted to get up, grabbing the sheet to cover herself.

"Where are you going?" Harry asked.

"I'm going to speak to my mother about this. Let go of the sheet." She huffed, tearing it away from Harry, who quickly grabbed the cover.

Harry laughed as she marched to the other side of the house to her parent's bedroom.

Shaking Victoria mildly, the girl whispered softly…

"Mother. MOTHER!"

Victoria awoke to find her daughter, Olivia, standing by her bedside with a bed sheet wrapped around her. She asked,

"Olivia, sweetheart, when did you get home?"

"Twenty minutes ago, and I find a naked man in my bed. What is he doing there?"

"Well, I should think he was sleeping until you so rudely woke him up."

"You had forgotten I was coming home from school, didn't you?"

"Yes, dear, on purpose."

"What do you mean, on purpose? I always come home from school." Olivia stated firmly, waking her father.

Chuck rolled over to see Olivia wrapped in the sheet. He asked, "Why are you wrapped in the sheet, honey? Your pajamas are in the dresser."

"I want to know why there is a man in my bed."

Being an occasional funny man, Chuck responds,

"Wedding present."

"Not funny, dad."

"Vicky, you handle it."

Victoria got up and walked Olivia to the bedroom. She knocked on the door and asked, "Harry, may I come in? It's Vicky." Harry quickly put some pants on and said,

"Yes, Vicky, come in. Is that crazy girl with you?"

"She'll stay out here for the moment. I want to ask if you wouldn't mind giving Olivia her bed for the evening? I have a most comfortable sofa in the living room I think you'll enjoy."

"I take it Olivia is not fond of the sofa," he joked.

"Get out of my bed, you creeping pervert!" Olivia said bursting into the room.

"Olivia, please. You told us you were coming home from school, and when did school end?" Vicky asked.

"In May." Olivia told her mother.

"Harry, what's today's date?"

"I believe we are in the middle of August. I'm not certain of the number on the calendar. But we are far away from May."

"Can you tell me why you didn't come home when you said you were going to?"

"I took a trip with some friends. We had the opportunity to fly to Barbados for a month's stay at a nature preserve."

"Was that with one of your professors, a teacher, perhaps a chaperone of sorts?" Vicky asked.

"No mother, just us four girls," Olivia confessed.

"Your father and I have some concerns about you, young lady. Where are the precautions you agreed to, about letting us know where you are, where you plan on going, especially for two months? Did you expect we would not worry about you? Do you think we are that callous with your welfare?"

"No mother. I'm sorry. I'll sleep on the sofa."

Harry jumped in. "Not with me you're not. I'd never get any sleep. You stay in the bedroom." Harry marched out to the sofa pretending not to care. He waited to see what Vicky would say when she exited the room.

Vicky approached Harry with a grin on her face. "I think you and I are going to get along very well, young man. If you find yourself free and need a wildcat to tame, I have one."

"Uh-huh. I can see that. I haven't had the opportunities with women as some of my peers have, and I've been grateful for it. It's been an education watching so many of them make fools of themselves." Harry paused a bit and asked Vicky,

"Can you sit awhile and talk? I know it's very late and we should all be asleep, but your daughter struck a spark in me I have never felt before. I'm not sure what I'm feeling, and I can't talk to my father about it. He's been gone a long time, and it's a time like this when I would surely want to talk to him." Harry said.

"You don't have complete trust and confidence in Jim yet, do you?" she asked.

"No, and I don't know why. Maybe it's because he and I haven't had those father-son get-togethers. I've been away at school, and my last two years were at Embry-Riddle in Florida. I should talk to my mother about these kinds of things but she's sleeping and to wake her would wake Jim and it was a long trip. I know they're both tired."

"Please don't get me wrong. I had some good times with some good friends down there, but nothing like the times I had with my dad. I miss him that much. And mom knows it."

"Now I'm trying to be the best I can be in my schooling and my dreams of a career in aviation engineering. I've passed all my flying courses with top grades. I have a private pilot's license, and an instrument rating, and night flying. I'm hoping to get my commercial license when I get to Prescott and delve a little deeper into the science of flight."

"So, I haven't spent a great deal of time with girls. I should admit I'm a little shy around them." Vicky jumped in…

"You were not shy about standing up to Olivia. I have never seen anyone do that to her before. You have a head start over any other boy she's brought home. Keep it up."

"That's funny you should say that. I think my mother would say the same thing, but she would also caution me to wait till after breakfast."

"Your mother would be right. That sounds like a good idea. Play the game soundly and don't let her attitude get in your head. Good night, Harry. See you in a couple of hours."

Harry sat up pondering what Vicky had told him. Not able to sleep he took the liberty of going to the fridge in search of a beer. He found one and went out to the pool patio. On the table he found a pack of cigarettes and took one. He sat back to watch the stars in the Louisiana sky, thinking of what his father would say to him, if he woke his mother what would she say. All he could hear was,

"You have to play the cards you've been dealt, Harry. Play it honestly, give everybody a fair shake, and just do the best you can…until your wings are done. I'll be waiting for you."

The screen door opened and gently closed, as if someone was trying to sneak up on him. He turned to see Olivia standing there with a chagrined look on her face. He asked her,

"I hope you have some clothes on under that sheet."

Olivia opened the sheet to show Harry she was still naked. Harry said, "You are shameless."

She walked over to the settee and sat next to him. Taking the cigarette from his lips she took a drag and handed it back to him. Then took the beer from his hand and took a long swallow.

Harry looked at her flashing, dark marble eyes. She waited for his first move. He didn't give her one, but he didn't ignore her. He put her aside and allowed her to play. But when she got too close with her advances he got up and began walking around. He told her,

"I can see you've had some experience teasing young men. You do it very well. I am not ashamed to admit I have not had the pleasure, and I am not going to start now with the daughter of my host. I might suggest you clothe yourself before your parents walk out here and find you in your birthday suit."

"I'm sorry," Olly said. "I don't do this on a regular basis. If you ask my friends, they will tell you I'm a stick-in-the-mud. I did take that trip to the Caribbean, but it wasn't to Barbados. I only got as far as the Keys." Olivia started to whimper. Harry let her go on.

"I ran out of money and was too ashamed to call home for more. I got a job waitressing in one of the restaurants down there and stayed with a couple of friends in a dumpy motel. I saved enough money for a bus ride home. It was such an awful experience that I can't tell my folks. They would yell and scream at me first and laugh at me later."

Walking over to her slowly, he stood over her as she sat wrapped in the bed sheet. He did not tell Olivia he had spoken to her mother, but he did say,

"I don't think they would do that. You did surprise a few people coming in the way you did. You certainly surprised me, but the way your mother managed it…I think it will all look different in the morning. Why don't you go to bed, get some sleep? Everybody will be up in a few hours."

"How about you?" Olivia asked.

"I'll be a minute. I need to digest a few things."

Harry walked around the pool, took off his pants and jumped in. He found the water refreshing in the southern heat and some clarity came to his mind. Around and around, he swam, thinking of what his father might say to him. After an hour, he climbed out of the pool, put his pants back on and walked back to the sofa to get more sleep. His father's words feeling like a good salve on a sore muscle.

The living room faced East, and Harry felt the heat of the rising sun coming in the window. Recognizing he was on the sofa and not in the bed, he got up and made his way to the bedroom. As he quietly opened the door, he could see Olivia was sleeping in the nude. Her back was to him, and he made the comment,

"Small butt."

He tip-toed in to get his underwear when Olivia woke. She turned over to see Harry searching through the clothes. As he turned toward her, she grabbed the sheet to cover up.

"You're up a little early," she said.

"The sun in the window started my day. I'm sorry I started yours. Go back to sleep. You have another hour before the others get up," he told her. "I'm glad you've found some modesty since yesterday."

"That was not intended, and you know it," she bit back.

"I know. I'm just kidding. No, I'm not. Get up and join me in the kitchen. We can start breakfast for everyone." Harry went into the kitchen in search of the utensils he would need. As he was going through the cabinets, Victoria walked in.

"Bacon and eggs, Harry? Or would you like a taste of the jambalaya I made yesterday?" she asked.

"Jambalaya. Yes, I would like a taste of Louisiana in the morning," he said excitedly.

Olivia came walking into the kitchen after slipping on a pair of short-shorts and a loose top. She watched her mother serve Harry a bowl of the Louisiana cuisine.

"Oh, mom. Can I have a bowl of jambalaya?" she asked taking a seat at the counter next to Harry.

Vicky looked back and forth between her daughter and Harry. "Is there a cease-fire between you two?"

Harry spoke up with surety, "Oh, yes. We talked a bit last night. Oh, and I grabbed a beer from the fridge last night."

"That's okay. You just enjoy your stay and help yourself while you're here." With motherly suspicion Vicky asked,

"So, what did you two talk about that put out the fire last night?"

"Just what kind of future we might be looking at after school," Olivia said.

"After last night I hope you do know, young lady, just where you are going when you graduate. Do you?"

"Not yet, mom. I'll have it figured out next semester." She turned to Harry and said, "I'm thinking of going for my Master's in Mathematical Engineering."

Harry's eyes went up, as well as Victoria's. Her mother asked, "That is quite a jump from Environmental Engineering, isn't it?"

"Well, I looked at the subjects and the course set-up and I've got most of them under my belt already. I figure I won't have too much trouble getting through."

"Do you enjoy math, Olivia?" Harry asked.

The long pause between bites of the spicy jambalaya made for some uncertainty as to the pause. Olivia was trying to think of a good answer. Knowing Harry was entrenched in math for his aviation stud-ies, she was now aiming to join him in Prescott, at Embry-Riddle. She didn't know how she was going to tell her parents, though.

"And what career path will that take you on?" Chuck asked, walking into the kitchen.

"Oh, you heard, Dad."

"Uh-huh. You've made this sudden change after meeting Harry by accident, for the first time last night?"

Shyly, Olivia didn't want to admit something had struck her last night, as much as it did Harry. "Yes," she answered.

"I think you should talk to your mother about some things, young lady. Things I can't talk to you about."

"Do you mean the birds and the bees, dad? I've got that solid. We covered that in science class."

"No, I mean about what you call love, and what we call love, and the differences between the two. But damn, it's too early for this."

CHAPTER 9

Olivia's Change

"Olivia? What are you doing? You can't make changes like this based on a feeling you got from someone. You need to keep your head in the game and stay on target. You had a goal to begin with and have come this far. Don't change it now because I'm here. You make it sound like I'm responsible for your actions, I'm not. Please think about this," Harry told her.

"Listen to Harry, honey," Vicky said. "Okay, suppose you follow Harry to Prescott to get a Master's in Mathematics, what are you going to do with it? It'll be aviation based; kind of limited, don't you think so?"

"No, mom. Dad, you tell her. The math I can use anywhere, in any field."

"That would be true, Vicky. But Olivia, sweetheart, do you really like aviation and planes and things? You've always thought I got carried away with my love of planes and the B-52s that come flying over the house. Now, because Harry shows up with Jim, you want to change your courses?"

"Yes, dad," Olivia answered plainly.

Chuck threw up his hands and said, "Well, it's not like you would be throwing your life away. You can use the math any-where. Have you called the school yet, to enroll?"

"Yes, but they said I needed a letter of recommendation from someone in the field, active or retired, because I didn't come out of their school in Florida. Can you write a letter for me, dad?"

"I think Jim would have more pull than me. He's an officer."

Jim and Liz got up when they heard the noise in the kitchen. He heard the conversation, and told Olivia,

"I would be happy to write a letter of recommendation for you. I know the air commander up there. I'm sure he'll let you enroll."

"Now what's for breakfast?" he asked. "I'll start with a coffee, please, Vicky?"

"You have a choice, Jim; a day old jambalaya or I can make up some bacon and eggs for you."

"I'll have the eggs, with toast if you don't mind. The grease on the bacon doesn't sit well in the morning. Later in the day it's a dif-ferent story."

All through breakfast Harry looked over at Olivia wondering if the girl had lost her mind. *Making a change like that because of me!* I cannot let her presence at school upset my plans. Dad said, 'play the cards you're given,' but I'm not sure I like this hand. He smiled at Olivia then called her outside toward the pool.

"I sure hope you know what you're doing, Olly."

"Olly? I like that," she said. "Call me that all the time, will you? It makes me feel special… to you."

"Oh, don't go mushy on me. We meet by accident in compro-mising positions, and you now want a life-long relationship. I can't do that right now, Olivia."

"Call me Olly," she insisted.

"Alright, Olly. We are going to have to maintain some sort of decorum, a set of rules, a separation, to keep us concentrated on our studies. At least I will have to do that."

Olivia looked at Harry and told him,

"I will do everything I can to maintain a sense of decorum, a separation, to let you concentrate on your studies…and me on mine."

"I am going to hold you to that, Olly," he said firmly.

It was still early in the day when breakfast ended. Chuck and Jim left Vicky with the mess and went out to the pool to join Harry and Olivia.

Looking at Harry, Chuck said, 'We can leave for the field anytime you're ready to rub the skin on a 52."

Harry was out of the pool as quick as Chuck finished his sentence. He ran into the house to dry off, change his clothes, and was standing by Jim in 15minutes.

"Did you want to see a B-52, Olly?" Harry asked.

She thought a bit then figured if she was going to bag Harry she had to get into his field. "Yes. Let me dry off and make a quick change." She zipped into the house, running by her mother and told her, "I'm going with dad, Jim and Harry."

Vicky looked at Liz and said, "She's going with Harry."

Jim looked at Harry and asked, "You call her Olly?"

"Yeah. My father once told me when you give something a name make it short. It's easier to remember and needs no explanation. Here she comes."

The four were ready to leave for the field when Vicky and Betty came running out of the house. "Wait. You're not going anywhere without us."

Chuck saw a need for something bigger than the Buick, so he went to the garage and brought out the Suburban.

"Now, everybody's got room, no squeezing or bunching up." He turned around to see Harry and Olivia sitting together in the third seat. "Comfy back there?" he asked facetiously.

Jim turned around waiting for an answer. Harry told him,

"Yes, Oh, yes," looking at Olivia.

Chuck showed his ID to the guard. Jim showed his, as well as Victoria and Olivia. Harry didn't have a dependents ID card, so he waited for the guard to fill out the paperwork to get Harry a pass.

Once given access, Chuck drove to the building where he would meet his contact.

As they exited the car, Jim spotted his old 52 parked and waiting for the order to go airborne. Some of the crew recognized him and came over to say hello.

"Colonel Perry, sir," Captain John Balls was now the pilot to Jim's ship. "Captain John Balls, sir, left seat to your old ride. Did you come in to see how we are handling her?"

"No. I know you fellas will take very good care of her. I'm here hoping to get this young man a look-see, maybe whet his whistle for a commitment. Harry Ackworth, Captain John Balls. He's the pilot on my old ride. He might be able to get you into the cockpit before I can."

"How did you get on base, Colonel?"

"Do you remember Chuck Gamer, my crew chief and radio man? He still has connections. Harry has been through Embry-Riddle's programs in Florida and is planning on continuing at the campus in Prescott. Aviation Engineering is what he's aiming for. Chuck said it was up to the high command, but he would do what he could to make things happen. I didn't expect to run into a crew."

"Things aren't much different since you retired, Colonel. A few upgrades to look at in the cockpit and tons of manuals to study on how they all work, but it's getting pretty intuitive. Lots of AI."

"That's what I want to get into, the AI," Harry told him.

"We have it, mister, and there is more coming. Have you gotten your private pilot's license yet?"

"Yes. I qualified on a Cessna 190 and got my instrument and night-time rating. I'm working on my commercial license and hoping to take the wheel of Jim's Lockheed Electra Junior. It is a beautiful airplane."

"I know that plane, Colonel. She flies very nicely. Wait here, would you?" The captain went into the hangar and came back followed by General George Hancock, commander of the base.

"Hello, son. So, you're Harry Ackworth. What was your father's name?"

"Donald Ackworth, sir."

"I believe I knew your father. I served with a Donald Ackworth in Viet Nam. In fact, he was the bombardier during operation Ranch Hand. I was radio. We flew quite a few missions together. Did he ever tell you what he did before you were born?"

"No. sir," Harry shook his head. "My father never mentioned he was in the service, let alone a bombardier on a 52. This is so ironic."

"And your mother hasn't said a word?" Jim asked.

"Not a word. Never. I wonder why?"

"I might know why." The General said to him. "Walk with me, son." Harry and the General walked into the hangar and made their way up to the General's office. He saw several photos hanging on the wall of Sergeant Hancock, now the General, posing in front of the B-52, *Winged One,* with Harry's father, Sgt. Donald Ackworth. Harry recognized his father immediately.

Harry said to himself, "This is why dad always said you're not going anywhere until your wings are done. If I may ask, General, how did you get from Sergeant to General?"

"If you stay in long enough, son, good things happen to you, and always for a reason. Your father and I always believed that. A mix up in orders came down and your father was supposed to be awarded the Distinguished Flying Cross. I was to get the Air Medal. We went up on one mission to bomb North Vietnam. One bomb got hung up on the rack. We couldn't stay that way for long."

"So, your father volunteered to go into the bomb-bay to free the bomb. It fell, almost taking him with it. He got hung up on the same rack the bomb got hung up on, and he couldn't get back in the plane. Part of his body was below the belly, and we couldn't close the doors."

"Your father and I were best friends for our whole tour. I was not going to watch him fall and have that dream in my head the rest of my life. I climbed down into the bomb-bay and wrapped a heavy wire around your father's foot, and I kept wrapping as far up his leg as I could. I would have wrapped his balls if I thought it would keep him from falling. I was strapped and latched and two crewmen behind me had hold of my belt so I wouldn't fall. Anyway, I yelled,

"On three! One -Two-Three, and I cut the hangar. Your father was flailing like crazy trying to reach for something to grabonto.

When he had a secure hold and was clearly inside, we closed the doors and got him back in the plane. That was the most courageous thing I had ever seen. When we got back to base our pilot put your dad in for the DFC and me for the Air Medal. When the award ceremony came, the orders got messed up and your dad got the Air Medal, and I got the DFC. We were told not to say a word. Your dad was rotated home, and the Air Force wasn't going to chase him down to give him his DFC."

"But let me tell you how happy I am that you are here.

"The Air Force did straighten out the crisscross of the orders and I surrendered the DFC and accepted my Air Medal. I told my commanding officer I would personally give Sergeant Donald Ackworth his DFC the next time I see him. I was sorry to hear he had passed away and I regret not making it to the funeral. But I have the honor of giving you your father's Distinguished Flying Cross for gallantry and bravery in the course of action against the enemy."

Harry was dumbfounded. "Dad was never a man to boast about any of his achievements, and that's why I never knew he was in the Air Force or did anything that would merit this award. Thank you, General. I have to show this to mom."

"You go out there and enjoy that B-52. The *Winged One,* I'm afraid, isn't with us anymore. But I personally penned your dad's name on the bomb-bay doors so any crew member would learn of his bravery. Take care, son."

"Thank you, General Hancock." Harry went back out on the tarmac and met with the pilot and Jim and Chuck. Olly, Vicky, and Liz stayed behind to watch the boys play with their toys and photographed the smiles on their faces when they came back to the car.

"Did you boys have fun?" Liz asked.

"It's been a long time, sweetheart, since I've been in one of those Beasts. I don't fit quite so well anymore." Chuck confessed.

"How about you, Jim? Was it worth it going back in time?" Liz asked.

"I can't say that it was. It's a young man's game any-more, and my memories will stay with the analog gauges, and not the digital clocks, dials and wiz-bang toys they've got up there. But it did bring back a lot of memories. How about you Harry? What struck you about the Beast?"

"Wait a minute," Olivia asked. "Why do you call a B-52 the Beast?"

Chuck pointed to the plane and said,

"Look at her. She's immense. The largest bomber in the world. She can do a hell of a lot of damage, and that's why they call her *The Beast*."

Harry was quiet and contemplative, looking like someone coming out of a dream, still lost. Olly touched his arm and asked,

"Tell us Harry, what struck you about the B-52?"

"My dad's name, on the bomb-bay doors, written where everyman can see it. They will learn what my father did at a time when it counted most." He turned to look at his mother, "and you didn't tell me, mom. Why?"

"I didn't know, Harry. Your father never spoke of his life before we married. It wasn't until the checks from the VA started arriving that I found out. Of course, it was too late to ask him then, and there was no one in the neighborhood I could talk to about it. So, I just accepted the money and put it away for your education. You didn't need to know. The insurance policy, on your father's death, also went for your college. That's all you needed to know. I couldn't tell you anything about his military time, I didn't know him then."

"We married several years later, when we met in college. Your father got his degree in Mechanical Engineering. I got mine in Nursing and we made our life together. Then you came along, and your father kept saying something, "I guess my wings aren't ready. I think I'll stick around a little longer."

As you grew the two of you developed such a close relationship. One time we thought we were going to have a second child, a baby girl, according to the doctor, and that she might spoil your relationship. But your father wasn't going to let that happen. "She will be your counterpart," he told me. But Georgia only lived a few months. She developed an illness and the doctors had nothing that would work against it.

"Your father was devastated, as was I, but we told ourselves we would go on and do for you as best we could, for you. Everyday your father would tell me he felt his wings were almost ready. I never knew what he was talking about until the day of the accident. I went to see him at the hospital. They told me he didn't have much time left.

He was facing the window watching a pair of mourning doves sitting side by side. He turned his face to me, told me he loved you and me, very much, but that his wings were ready. He pointed to the window, and when the birds were gone, there remained two pure white wing feathers, one left and one right. I opened the window and picked them up. When I turned to give them to your father, he was gone. I still have those feathers, son. They are the most precious gift your father ever gave me. They will be yours one day, Harry. Now you understand your father's reference of the wings. But I never knew he spent any time in the Air Force."

Harry opened the medal case General Hancock gave him and showed her the shining Distinguished Flying Cross his father was awarded so long ago.

"The General told me why dad was awarded the medal." Harry told the story to everyone on the way home.

"That's quite an honor, Harry. It's high on the list of medals the Air Force gives. You should be very proud."

"I am. I always have been. Now, I always will be, even more so."

CHAPTER 10

Leveling Off

Their visit was a long four days. Liz, Harry and Jim had done what they had come for and more. Harry found out that his father was near to being a hero and he told no one. But that's what live heroes do. Their exploits go untold unless told by someone else. In this case it was a firsthand witness who blew the whistle on Donald Ackworth.

It was the right award given to the wrong man, but 40 years later, the right man gets the right award, posthumously, by his service buddy. It's crazy to think the Air Force can't make a mistake, they do. Consider how large they are. Mistakes are bound to happen. But Don Ackworth is no longer with us, so his son will have the honor of thinking better of his father.

Now there's a new semester beginning and a new problem, a female problem. Chuck Gamer's daughter, Olivia. Supposedly smitten, bitten by the love bug, and very willing to change her life's path to pursue a relationship with Harry.

How does Harry feel about it? He is not ready for any kind of relationship with anyone. Trying to make Olivia under-stand is like trying to empty Niagara Falls with a teaspoon. Now he has to say goodbye as he heads off to school in Arizona. Olivia has told her parents she wants to move to Arizona and change her curriculum to attend school in Prescott where Harry will be.

Chuck wished Jim all the success in the world with his new plane, and to Harry, he said he and Victoria would pray for him. They knew Olivia had plans to follow him to Prescott.

Harry felt the ride to the airport seemed longer than when they first arrived. "We're not in the air, yet?"

Time felt like it was standing still. He wanted to go home and get away from the shock of Olivia's presence in his life.

"What do I do now, dad? We never talked of something like this coming up. We never really talked of women and the effect they can have on your life, the dreams, the plans you make for your future."

"Just play the cards you're dealt, son, as best you know how, and life will follow."

His father's words were never far from Harry's mind, and they always brought him solace. On the flight home he switched places with his mother so she could sit up front next to Jim. The back seat was spacious enough for him to lounge a bit. There was a need for him to be alone with his thoughts. Now, if he only had a beer and a cigarette...

Liz stared at the instruments in front of her and braced her inner-self against the protruding buttons, dials and toggle switches, the video screens, and the funny looking broken yoke. The colors, red, yellow, green; all having a meaning of their own, not a Christmas tree decoration. It was all a go and stop light of what to do and what not to do at the right or wrong time.

"Ah, Jim?" Liz asked. "You know what all these dials and switches are for?"

"Yes, I do, dear." he said, sounding prideful.

"It all appears so daunting, I know, but you can't take it in all at once. It is simply a redundancy of one system. Don't forget, there are two engines out there, so each must have its own set of instruments. And then there are the separate instruments that are common to both the pilot and the co-pilot. It isn't something you learn. It does take practice and lots of it."

"And you've been flying for how many years, Jim?"

"My father introduced me to flying when I was 12. He was in the Army Air Corps. We lived right off base in Dayton, Ohio and I got to see planes all the time. My first flight was in an open cockpit Stearman."

"You mean one of those old planes with no cover over you?"

"Uh-huh, open cockpit. Oh, I was scared at first. All the noise and the wind as we rolled down the runway, and it was bumpy. Then dad pulled back on the stick and we climbed up and up until he let off the throttle and we just cruised with the engine thrumbling along at a steady rpm. It was great. I can still remember it."

"You make it sound so exciting, especially for a 12 year-old." She looked about the cabin and said, "Now you've grown to something as complex as."

"This isn't complex, dear. The B-52 is complex. In front of me I have everything I need to fly this plane, including the radio. In the 52, I have to know what's going on with 8 jet engines and each system for that engine. My radio in the 52 is just a small outlet to the one sitting below me in a room crowded with many radios and listening devices. The Navigator sits next to the radio man and his board is just as complex."

"The flight engineer bounces all over the plane to make sure all the systems are working properly and jumps in to fix it if one goes off-line or malfunctions. The co-pilot sits next to me and plays solitaire waiting for my instructions."

"That's not true," Liz says with surprise.

"No, it's not. His job is just as important as mine. He is my right hand, keeping me informed of any irregularities in the cabin I might miss." Jim leans over and kisses Liz by surprise and tells her, "You're funny."

After 800 miles Jim landed in Wilmington, N.C. While the Lockheed was being refueled, they walked the terminal in search of a restaurant with a varied menu.

"Do you feel like anything special, Liz?" Jim asked.

"No, not really. A good sandwich would do me."

"How about you, Harry?" His mother asked. She turned around to find Harry standing in front of a pizza restaurant reading the menu board.

"Is that what you want, Harry, pizza?" she asked.

"Yeah. I haven't had a pizza in a while, and I've never had southern pizza. I think I'll give it a try."

Jim and Liz looked at one another and said, "Okay."

After two hours of pizza and Coke they walked back to the hangar to find *Ginny's Gin* serviced and ready for the trip home. In the air Harry sat up front with Jim and the two talked of the experience in the -52, the coming semester at Embry-Riddle's Prescott, Arizona campus, and the target Harry was aiming for after graduation.

"I want to get into the future of commercial aviation. I see the plane not only getting bigger and faster but reaching higher into the atmosphere. That will involve greater risks, more complexity for the airframe, the pilot, and the passengers. The systems we use to make those leaps will change. It could involve a greater use of electricity for propulsion, with complex battery structures, the use of Hydrogen as a fuel, or even solar. And it will mean more schooling, beyond a Masters, diving deeper into the engineering."

"That's a very heady dream, Harry. Are you sure you're ready for that? Don't forget, Olivia is tugging at your coat tails."

"I can't think of that, Jim. Olly has no dream to leave her mark in life, to do something that can be effective in people's lives."

Liz spoke up. "She's a lovely girl whose met her equal. You gave her a challenge, Harry, when you two bumped heads in the middle of the night. Neither of you would come to understand what it all meant for some time, but everything happens for a reason."

"You're not telling me that I'm supposed to marry that 'lovely girl,' are you mom? I find her too forward, even if she calls it a cover-up."

"What do you mean a cover-up, Harry?"

"Ollie said if I asked her friends about her, they would say she was a stick-in-the-mud. And she also admitted to me, not telling her parents, that her escapade to Barbados ended up in a restaurant in the Keys, trying to earn enough money for a bus ticket home. If that's not a wild and unpredictable nature?"

"Harry, Olivia is still young, and Chuck and Vicky may have given her a free rein in her upbringing. She needs direction and I think she's looking for it. I think she sees the happiness in her folks lives and wants the same thing. And she's not without a dream, Harry. She has a target, the Environment, isn't that what she said?"

"Yeah, Environmental Engineering, but I don't think Embry-Riddle is going to give her that, mom. It's an aviation school."

"She's doing that to be next to you, Harry, and I should find that complimentary, and exciting…another challenge for you."

"Even dad would not have taken on that kind of challenge, mom."

"Oh, but he did, Harry. He did."

"How do you mean? I saw our lives as good and happy ones. Dad never looked like he was battling two things at once, and nothing that was too daunting. He always came out ahead. You both did."

"I guess I should tell you something your father asked me not to tell you." his mother was confessing.

"What, mom? A family secret, you want to tell me now. Mom, I'm 22 years-old, what is going to make a difference now?"

"I saw you were so happy with your father while you were growing up, and he felt it, too. He couldn't bring himself to tell you he was sick inside. He had been for a very long time. He told me before we married, and I married him anyway. Your father was my perfect husband, regardless of any flaw's others' might have seen, and I wasn't going to let him go. He accepted that knowing I accepted the unknown time limit we would have together. We checked with doctors, and they told us what your father had was not hereditary, so you don't have it."

"What is it, mom? What did dad have and where did he get it?"

"Your father volunteered to work on the nuclear weapons projects the Air Force was involved with. They found he was exposed to a high amount of radiation somehow and told him the exposure was terminal. They just couldn't tell him how long he had. You had 15 good years with your father, and I had three more. So, for all your life, your father was battling the effects of the radiation sickness; dealing with his job at the plant, things at home, making sure he spent quality time with you and me. The doctors found he had a massive heart attack at the time of the accident. He could have died when the accident happened, but he didn't. He waited to say goodbye."

The lack of conversation in the cabin made the engine's thrumming more pronounced.

"I guess it wouldn't have made any difference if you had told me. Dad would not have accepted any kind of sympathy or caring assistance from anyone, not even you and I," Harry said softly.

"I hope you're not angry with me, Harry, are you?"

"No, mom. I suppose I should be but telling me wouldn't have done any of us any good. I understand why you or dad didn't tell me. Really, I do." Harry paused for a while before asking,

"But what has that got to do with how I'm supposed to handle Olly?"

"Olly? Oh, you've already given her a nick-name. That right there shows you care, Harry," his mother told him.

"Mom. It's a nick-name, nothing more."

"And every time you see her from now on, you will call her Olly, not Olivia. Wait and see."

"Your mother's right, son. And who could argue with their mother…and win?" Jim added.

Harry expelled a puff of air and finished the Olly conversation with, "Dad always said, play the cards you're dealt and play fairly. Your wings will come when they're done. I guess that's all I can do."

The remainder of the flight home was pointing out the scenery below and testing the geographical knowledge of the three of them. Jim usually knew where he was but sometimes got the area wrong. Harry would correct him, and Liz would act as referee.

It was almost 9:00PM when they landed at North Central in Lincoln, Rhode Island. Jim taxied the Electra to its hangar at the far end of the runway and parked it for its next round of service. Jim's car was waiting where he first parked it and he drove Liz and Harry home. He was going to drive back to his apartment in East Providence when Harry asked,

"Why don't you stay here tonight?"

"That's funny coming from you, Harry. I would expect your mother to say something like that, not you."

"I would, I mean, I haven't asked because I know you enjoy the privacy in your own apartment, and I don't mind." Liz told him.

Harry added, "I think your relationship with my mother is no secret and shows nothing is lacking between you two. Why keep a separate apartment when you could put the money in the plane? I don't think mom would object to your moving in, would you, mom?"

"You're embarrassing me now, Harry. No, I would not mind. Stay the night and you can pick up your things tomorrow and move in here, with us."

"At least until I go off to college," Harry told them. "I'm going to bed. Good night, mom, Jim."

CHAPTER 11

The Books, Maybe

Harry's father's car lay undercover in the garage. It was a 1958 Oldsmobile needing a little TLC. It ran well but Jim looked at it before Harry left for Prescott.

"It sounds okay, Harry, but, if you don't mind, I would like to give it a tune up and check a few other things to make sure it's safe for the long ride to Prescott. Your mother and I want to do what we can to keep you safe even though the biggest part of that is your job, now."

"Thanks, Jim. I really appreciate it. Do you think you and mom might fly out to Prescott, this fall? For a visit…on your way to the coast?"

"Who said we were going to the coast, Harry?"

"Mom."

"Oh, she saw my dream sheet. Well, it was going to be a surprise, something for the both of us to enjoy before the winter set in. Yes, Harry, I think we can do that. But we don't want you to wait for us. Concentrate on your studies and get your plans in action. Play your hand, as your dad would say."

"I'll do that. Thanks for the help with the car, and thanks for the advice, and treating my mom so special. She deserves it."

"Yes, she does," Jim affirming his love and caring for Liz.

Harry left for Embry-Riddle's second campus on a Wednesday morning. The Old's was prepped, washed, and packed for school. He had the money he needed for the motels and the route mapped out for the shortest, fastest way to Prescott, Arizona.

"Bye, mom, Jim. I'll call when I arrive and get settled in. I may call along the way. See ya."

Harry pulled out of the driveway onto Scott Road and made his way south to the George Washington Highway to make the connection onto I-295 South to meet up with Interstate 95. He followed it West to Port Chester, Connecticut and jumped onto 287 West, through White Plains, NY, and across the Tappan Zee Bridge. In Suffern, NY he turned South onto 287 to pick up I-78 and the beginning of the long trip across the country to Prescott, AZ.

When he hit Harrisburg, PA he saw Jim had plotted a route south on I-81, and a stop in Staunton, Virginia. There he would have his evening meal and sleep over. In the morning the map showed a plot to stay on 81 to Knoxville, Kentucky then pick-up I-40 West, across to Flagstaff, down I-17 to Prescott and a couple of smaller roads through the Prescott National Forest. The 3000 mile journey was not an inexpensive one, but Harry had a gas card from Jim that took care of the car's thirst.

He was given the tour of the campus with all the other students in the Aeronautical courses. The airfield was only four miles from the campus and had several dozen planes, large and small, private and commercial, parked all around the campus at various hangars. He was excited and felt his confidence grow that he would receive the kind of education he wanted in his c hosen field.

He thought for a moment of what Olivia might do if she were there. "There's nothing here for her as far as Environmental Engineering is concerned. I'm glad she stayed in Louisiana, or wherever she was going to school. I won't have to bother her, and she won't bother me."

Campus housing was as comfortable as any school can provide and not a far walk to the classrooms. Coming and going from the dorm to the classroom to the airport was done by shuttle bus. They were allowed to use their own cars, but Harry decided to let the school pay for the gas and use the shuttle bus.

The days in the classrooms flew by and the classes at the airport just weren't long enough, for Harry. He enjoyed the firsthand instructions with the various airplanes, in the engine bays and the airframes. He absorbed every word and every moment with the scratch sheet and a pencil, or with a wrench. His instructors were impressed with his ability to grasp everything so quickly. They didn't have to wonder of his ability behind the wheel. From the ground to the sky, Harry proved he could fly an airplane with confidence.

In his mailbox one morning and found a letter from Carnegie Mellon University, hand-written in a very pretty script. "Wow, this looks interesting." He sniffed the envelope to smell for perfume but there was none.

"I don't know anyone at Carnegie Mellon," he thought, slitting the letter open. Then a big grin came across his face. It was from Olivia Gamer.

"Son-of-a-gun," he exclaimed. He began to read

> *"Harry, I want to apologize for the fool I made of myself during your visit to my parent's place in Shreveport. I must admit I did enjoy your company. I must also admit you did something to my heart, something I have never felt before, but that I want to feel again.*
>
> *Our first meeting was a shock to the both of us, but the shock wore off and the feeling of welcome replaced it. Then there was that feeling of want. I did not understand why you didn't respond, until my parents told me of your father and all you shared with him, how he was the center of your universe. He taught you about dedication and a stick-to-attive attitude with an emphasis on fair play, and something about the cards you are dealt. You will have to explain that to me one day.*

I am writing to say I miss you. I want to be with you again, to go where you go, and be there when you need someone. I don't think you want to hear that four letter word, not from me right now, and maybe you're not ready to use it either. I'll hold onto mine, but could I ask you to hold onto yours?

I'm being a silly girl right now, smitten and blind with only one vision. My mother told me these feelings I'm having are not unlike the one's she felt for my father when they first met, and they have been together for more than 40 years.

Can we do that, Harry?

If you think I'm being too forward, again, please let me know. If you want me to stop bothering you and writing to you, tell me also and I will stop. But I will not stop missing you and feeling this way about you.

Good luck in school,

Endearing forever,
Ollie XO"

Harry was stunned but stunned with a smile. As he read the short letter, he began to feel that certain something he felt after his interaction with Olly. His mother, Betty, told him she felt that indescribable feeling when she met Harry's father.

"But we spent so little time together, how could I feel something for her so quickly? We hardly know each other, and I wasn't ready to explore her charms as she pretended I could. A stick-in-the-mud? Her friends may be right, but not to the degree they would tell of her." He began to rub his chest feeling something was going on.

CHAPTER 12

A Lovely Interruption

"OO! That almost hurts. I wonder what that is?"

The feeling subsided when it was time to get to class. But all day it kept gnawing at him, and all day he kept rubbing his chest. The instructor noticed his discomfort and asked,

"Are you alright Harry?"

"Just a little indigestion from breakfast, sir. It'll pass."

That feeling didn't pass and Harry took a walk to the dispensary. The doctor examined Harry and took some blood. He got into a conversation on how Harry's classes were going.

"The classes are going very well. I'm very happy with my selection of subjects, my course outline. My goal hasn't changed, yet."

"What do you mean yet, Harry? Are you having a change of mind in attending the school?"

"Oh, no. It's an outside thing that has me wondering about tomorrow." Harry explained.

"How so? You are sure to have employment somewhere in the aviation field almost anywhere around the world. Isn't that why you came to Embry-Riddle in the first place?"

"Yes, it is, but…"

"But what has you thinking twice about it now?"

Shyly he told the doctor, "A girl."

"Ah!" the doctor said, putting away his tools.

"I know now the cause of your discomfort, young man."

"You do?" He looked at the doctor and surrendered,

"Aw, doc, don't tell me it's the girl. I don't need to hear that when I'm trying to set up a career. No, don't do it, doc."

"Can't help it, Harry." The Doctor looked at him and asked, "Did you talk to anyone else about this? Your mother, maybe?"

"Yes, before I left for school, but that was 6 months ago."

"Uh-huh. Sometimes our hearts don't recognize what our mind is seeing. In other words, the plans for your future have clouded your natural instincts. Let me ask you…when was the last time you had sexual relations with a girl?"

Embarrassed, Harry tried to shy away from answering the question. He finally said, "I haven't had relations with a girl yet. But that doesn't mean I haven't been approached."

"So, you're a virgin." The doctor remarked. "That is a rare state to be in Harry, at your age. I congratulate you. This girl that is bothering you now. Did she try to get you to go to bed with her?"

"Not really, I mean she did get, 'cozy', if that's the right word, But I didn't give her a positive response."

"Why not? Are you gay?" The doctor was being point blank with Harry.

"You ask the same questions my father would be asking."

"Would be? You haven't talked to him about these things?"

"My father has been gone since I was 15. He died in an accident. We got to talk about a lot of things, but sex and girls was not one of them."

"And, of course talking to your mother about those things is way out of line."

"Yes. You know it is. A guy can't talk to his mom about that. We can talk about girls but not about sex."

"Hm, well, if you don't mind an old doctor's perspective, do you mind if I play your father? I mean, I hate to see nice guys like you get hurt. You are not the first young man I've talked to about the ways of young ladies, their raging hormones, and what a virile young man should do when confronted with such a predicament."

"And?" Harry asked.

"Well, to be wise about the whole thing, measure what she wants, not what you can give her. If it's only sex, odds are you're in for trouble. If she starts out looking for someone to talk to, a friend, and she expresses that she likes you, well, play your cards carefully, fairly."

"Wow! That is exactly the way my father would have said it…'Play your cards carefully and fairly.' He alwayse alwsy told me you have to play the cards yo said you have to play the hand you're dealt in life. I was never sure what that meant, but I hear it allot so I guess it means something."

"I think I would have liked your father. I'm sorry he's not here to give you advice. I'll give you what I can, when and if you are looking for it. Right now, I'm pretty sure that pain is a 'love' pain, even if you won't recognize it, and it is not going away, son. You will have to find a way to deal with it."

Those were the doctor's last words as Harry left his office. He kept patting the letter in his pocket. It made the pain in his chest subside so he could concentrate on his classes. He said to himself,

'Maybe there is something between Ollie and me.'

Harry finished his classes for the day and felt good about how they went. But now it was time to deal with Ollie and to discuss with her what she expects from a relationship with him. He didn't have her phone number, but he did have her address at Carnegie Mellon. He found some parchment paper among his supplies.

"Mom must have wanted me to write something special. Nice paper. I'll use a page or two to write to Ollie."

Ollie received the letter with a return address of Embry-Riddle University, Prescott, Arizona.

"Oh, boy! I wasn't expecting this so soon," she thought. She admired the paper Harry had chosen and the long-hand script he used to write in.

"Harry's got nice penmanship," she noticed. Opening the letter, she read,

Dear Ollie,

Your letter caught me by surprise. After 6 months, I didn't expect to get a letter. I thought perhaps you had forgotten about me. Your apology was not necessary. After rationalizing the conditions under which we met, and your activity in the pool, I've come to conclude, "You have a small butt." Ha-Ha!

If I have to be as serious as I was at your parents' home, then I have to meet this pain in my chest head on. I didn't know what it was, where it came from or how it got there, so I went to the doctor. Do you know what he said it was?

"It is a resultant anomaly that is acquired from contact with a member of the opposite sex. A non-physical interaction creating an unexplainable harmonic resonance that supersedes the natural positioning of the stars and the alignment of hormonal vibrations in the human body."

Actually, that was scientific bullshit, those are my words. The doctor used the word, Love!

I told him it couldn't be, that I could not afford to get involved with a woman at this time. I was too busy making my career. You see, my dad never told me anything about this stuff. He was too busy making his career, so the doctor filled in for him, telling me the only conclusion he could come up with was love. What I was experiencing was the prick from that little prick Cupid and his dumb arrows. Dad told me to deal with it, and like he said, "play the hand you're dealt and play it honestly."

Okay. I guess I'll have to dive right into this. There is no getting away from the pain in my chest unless you are here with me. The pain only goes away when I'm holding your letter.

If you seriously want to change your major and join me here in Prescott, be well prepared to work hard. In school you will get your hands dirty, your knuckles scraped and look down at the world from 10,000 feet because you will do some flying. I will personally take you up in a Cessna 152 to get you ready to handle the controls. You will have to learn total concentration because it is a life saver in the air. You will also learn spatial recognition to adapt to different heights above the ground.

One very important part to all of this…you and I will have to learn to study together, work together, live together. My dorm is on the first floor, and I have the room to myself. We can make it work if we learn to work together. I will speak to my headmaster about getting a place for you, but I would prefer we lived together, not apart, as in a co-ed dorm. I don't want to try any other way. I think it would be too distracting, thinking of you all the time, so near, but not able to touch you. And we would be living on the cheap.

But of course, it all depends on you. I am writing with the prospect that everything you did at your parent's home was for a good reason. Being here with me was something you wanted to do and now I want it, too. Come to Prescott!

Harry OOXOO

Ollie was scared, she didn't know what to do. She called her parents to explain to them that she had written and what Harry wrote back. She wanted advice. Chuck deferred to Vicky and went out to the pool.

"You made Harry uncomfortable when you first met, Olivia."

"Mom, we were both naked, and we didn't know each other. Could we be more uncomfortable at that time? I think not."

"Alright, you may be right on that one, but Harry never chased you or tried to coerce you into doing something you did not want to do. Did he?"

"So why does he now want me to live with him? I send him one letter of apology and he goes all a-twitter."

"It had to be what you wrote, or did you perfume the letter?" Vicky asked.

"No perfume, mom, just an honest apology for making him feel uncomfortable."

"So, that pain you felt when Harry was here is now gone?" "No, I still get it, every time I think of him. And though I have dated other boys on campus, none have been able to erase the pain. They cannot take Harry's place, mom."

"Well," Vicky declared, "I just heard the answer to your problem. Do you want to wait till September and the beginning of the next semester? Or do you want to see him now and move your stuff in at the end of this semester? You don't have a great deal of things to move. We can do it in one trip and with the Suburban. You have till supper to make up your mind."

She strolled out to the pool and never stopped. Walking past her father she jumped in and let the water engulf her, allowing her to sink into its watery arms.

Chuck watched her, floating just below the surface, not swimming. He turned around to see Vicky walking out to him.

"What is it, hon? Why is she bothered by him? She has never had this kind of trouble with a boy before. Why Harry?"

"Why is it you and I, dear? Do you remember how we met? We didn't know what we were doing that first night you kissed me."

"No, dear. You kissed me first." Chuck pointed out to her.

"Okay, I kissed you first. But we were just as confused then as she is now. In matters of love, time hasn't changed a thing. She felt that strange pain when Harry was here. Now Harry is feeling that same strange pain. They have something between them that says they are meant to be together. No man or science can break that connection."

"Now, you're going too far, dear."

"Oh, okay, but you know what I mean. We had it and now they have it. "

"So, what do you think we should do?" Chuck wondered.

"I think we should take her to Prescott and let her and Harry sort it out. It's the only way they're going to know for sure. If it doesn't work out, then it wasn't meant to be. But right now, I think it's the only way Olivia is going to find the answer to what she's feeling."

"Should I give her my perspective? Do you want me to talk to her?" Chuck asked.

"A father's view of the heart?" Vicky asked. "I don't think that would be a bad idea. Why don't you?"

Chuck tried to call Olivia out of the pool. When she wouldn't answer him, he got down to his skivvies and went in. Olivia looked up at her father and went to him for a hug.

"I know you're confused right now, honey, but can we talk about this outside the pool?" He mused.

Olivia nodded and the two got out of the water to sit on the deck. Vicky brought out two towels and the three of them sat at one of the tables and began to discuss what Olivia might want to do. Chuck lit a cigarette and placed it in the ashtray. Olivia took the cigarette and took a drag. Her parents were surprised to see Olivia with a cigarette.

"Do you do that regularly?" Vicky asked.

"No." Olivia answered. "It depends on the circumstances. Harry does the same thing."

"Oh," Chuck remarked. He looked at her and asked,

"What do you think you would like to do?"

"On one hand I want so bad to see him again. On the other, I'm afraid I might be taking a 1000 mile trip just to say hello."

"Harry's letter…he did say he wanted you to come to Prescott. It sounds to me like he wants to try to start something with you, but he's leaving the final decision up to you." Chuck told her.

"And that's heavy, dad. I don't know if I can make that kind of decision. Not now, anyway."

"Then, you have to tell Harry, again, how you feel, right now. If you can't decide, then I think that pain was simply indigestion. Because real love pain can only be satisfied when the two of you are together. Tell him you need more time or tell him you are on your way up. Your mother and I will back you all the way, and I don't mind a road trip," Chuck grinned.

"I would like to talk to him, but I don't have his phone number." Olivia said.

"I'll call Jim and get it." Chuck called Jim and got Harry's dorm number.

"What's going on, Chuck?" Jim asked.

"It seems there a pains in the kids' chests that a doctor can only describe as a love pain, and Harry is asking Olivia to come to Prescott to ease that pain. Olivia can't make up her mind how to fix it."

"Did this come about from a letter one of them sent?" Jim asked.

"Yes. How did you know?"

"I've been there, Chuck. It was many years ago, but I was there once, too. I seem to remember a certain Tech Sergeant I had. He had this bad habit of always reading the same letter over and over again, carried it with him on every flight. He just could not put the letter down. He had this 'pain' in his chest. It almost got him grounded." Jim told him.

"Yeah...I remember, and I married the girl that wrote the letter. Thanks for the memory, Colonel, and the phone number."

"Anytime, Sergeant," Jim answered.

Chuck handed the phone number to Olivia. "Here's your starting point, hon." He looked at Vicky and they went into the house to leave her alone with the man on the other end of the line.

CHAPTER 13

New Decisions

The phone in the hallway of the Hangar Dorm, rang four times as Harry was walking by it. He picked it up, 'Hello,' he answered with a smile.

"May I speak to Harry Ackworth, please?"

Harry paused, recognizing it was Ollie, composing what he would say. He began simply, "Ollie?"

"Harry?" She waited for Harry to start the conversation. The silence between them seemed to go on forever.

"I got your letter, Harry. I think we need to discuss this, my moving up there, I mean."

"But you said you were going to change your Major and was willing to come up to Prescott. Are you changing your mind?"

"I'm confused, Harry. I don't know what I want to do now."

"Is there someone else, Ollie? You can tell me. If there is, I hope it stops this crazy pain I have. If there isn't, then I guess I'll have it until you get here. I need you, Ollie…I want you. I don't know if that's what they call love. If it is, then…I love you."

Olivia stopped and didn't say anything. Struck by three simple words… *"I Love You"…he said. A boy I meet accidentally, naked, in the middle of the night, and something is happening.*

"What the hell is it?" She wondered what was she supposed to do? Her mother came out of the bedroom carrying two suitcases. Olivia looked and asked,

"Where are you going, mom?"

"Your father and I are taking a road trip up to Prescott, Arizona to see Harry. Do you want to come?"

"Talk about having decisions made for you," Olivia told her. She said to Harry, "I must go, Harry. Make room for me."

"I'll be there in two days." And she hung up.

Harry looked at the phone, "What the hell…and she's coming up, in two days. She'll be here in two days!" he realized. "I'm glad it's the weekend. This is going to be wild."

Chuck picked up the phone as he, Vicky and Olivia were heading out the door. "Hello."

"Chuck, it's Jim. How did things work out for the kids?"

"Filled with confusion, Jim. Vicky and I are making the choice for Olivia by taking her up to Prescott. She and Harry will have to work it out face to face."

"So, when are you leaving?" Jim asked.

"We were headed out the door when you called."

"Oh, well. Liz and I will jump in the Electra and meet you there. I know they have a nice airstrip at the school. See you Sunday, sergeant."

Jim and Liz packed some clothes. He called the air strip to have the plane ready and they were in the air in less than an hour.

"This is going to be fun," Jim told Liz.

"So, we're going to Prescott to watch Harry and Olivia settle something?"

Jim told her all Chuck told him about the letters passed between their children; that Harry wants Olivia to move to Prescott, enroll in Embry-Riddle, and move in with him.

Liz stiffened up in her seat and said,

"That is about as far from the Harry I know that I want to get. Does that sound like a proposal to you, Jim?"

"Yes, it does deary. Yes, it does." Jim looked at Liz and surprised her with, "Liz, will you marry me?"

Liz's eyes opened as wide as her eyes could get. Her jaw dropped for a moment and then she smiled. A calm washed over her, as Jim watched the skies, darting back and across the instruments. He waited an eternity for her answer. 30 seconds later Betty looked up and said, quietly,

"Yes, Colonel James Perry. I will."

Jim reached into his vest pocket and pulled out a 1 carat diamond ring. It was white gold with a silver cradle mounting a beautifully cut stone, and, somehow, it was the right size.

"How did you know what size?"

"I hired a private investigator to find out," he told her.

"You did not," she slapped his sleeve.

"No, Harry told me, when he was home last."

"And you've been holding on to it for a month? When were you going to ask me?"

"When the time was right. I didn't expect it to be at 10,000 ft., but what the heck. It worked."

"So, Harry knows about the engagement?" she asked.

"No. He thinks I'm just buying you a nice ring."

"Well, I must say, it is a very nice ring."

"You know we are going to have to stay one night somewhere. St. Louis has a nice regional airport east of the river. We can find a place to stay there for the night."

It was 1000miles to St. Louis and they had been in the air long enough. It was time to walk around a bit and stretch their legs. The Electra drew a crowd around the hangar where Jim parked. Mechanics and pilots from around the airport came by to gaze at the antique beauty. The crew chief that night came by to greet Jim and Liz. Jim gave him the key and told him to service it for tomorrow's flight.

After finding out there were no hotels, motels, or B&B's, immediately around the airport, they rented a car and found a Marriott in the middle of the city. Liz enjoyed the excitement and bustle of the big city. A fitting engagement dinner that night, some personal moments in the later evening, and a delicious breakfast in the morning made for a great flight coming up.

The Electra was fueled and prepped and greatly admired by the ground crew. Recalling Emilia Earhart and her association with St. Louis, the crew prepped the plane with all the love the relic deserved. Jim and Liz boarded, plotting a course to Embry-Riddle and Prescott, AZ, 1200 miles away.

Jim didn't notice when they boarded, but during the flight a cooler had slid across the cabin floor. He wondered where it came from. Betty picked it up and opened it to find two sandwiches and a thermos of hot coffee with two cups. A note inside read.

> *"Thanks for gracing St. Louis Regional Airport with*
> *your Lockheed Electra 12-A. She's a beautiful relic*
> *of days gone by, days many of us still long for.*
>
> *The cooler you can return on your next stop.*
> *Thanks again,*
> *The Ground Crew"*

Jim laughed and then wiped his eyes at the gesture, the care and the dedicated service they performed on his plane.

"I guess we'll have to go back to St. Louis to return the cooler, huh?"

"I'm game to go wherever you go, Jim Perry," Betty told him.

"It's a date," he added.

CHAPTER 14

A Hug, A Kiss

Chuck's GPS was programed to take him across the desert of the Texas Panhandle. It was almost 500 miles to Lubbock, and though the Suburban returned decent gas mileage, he was going to try to stop for fuel anywhere he could. His plan worked and he pulled into a motel in Lubbock with fuel to spare. It would be another 600 miles to Prescott, but this part of the journey was going to take him over some low mountains and the car would be using more fuel. He marked Socorro, NM as a place to stop and gas up.

As Navigator and Flight Engineer on a B-52 George knew how to plot a course and keep it economical and fuel efficient. The Hampton Inn was the first motel he came to and was the place to stop. He still had fuel in the tank and felt proud that he hadn't forgotten how to calculate fuel consumption. The ladies got out to stretch their legs before going into the room.

Olivia made a dash to the phone to call Harry. It was nearing the supper hour but all she was hungry for was to hear Harry's voice.

"Hello," he answered.

"Harry? It's Ollie, I'm in Prescott, at the Hampton Inn. Where can I meet you tonight?" Olivia was filled with expectation and excitement.

"Ah, I don't know. I don't get out much, so I don't know the town, well. Tell your dad to take 69 to the intersection across from the Hilton. There's a parking lot behind the hotel. I'll be parked in there somewhere. What is he driving?"

"The white Suburban," Ollie tells him.

"Okay, that'll be easy to spot." Not too many Suburban's around here, he thought. "I'll see you in the parking lot in 30 minutes."

Harry drove to the parking lot to meet up with Ollie and her mom and dad. He spotted them waiting in one corner. When he pulled up in his Old's, Chuck asked where he had gotten it and how he was able to keep it running all these years.

"It was my dad's, parked in the garage. I found it under a canvas cover. Jim and I did some work on it before I left."

Harry had just finished answering Chuck when Ollie walked up to him and said shyly, "Hi. How are you?"

"I am doing much better now that you're here."

Ollie smiled and put her arms around him. Harry reciprocated and gave her a big hug. Then he planted a big kiss on her and she came back with one for him. After a minute, Vicky suggested,

"Harry, Olivia…come up for air, will you please? It's embarrassing for your father and I to be standing out in a parking lot while you two lock lips."

Harry unlocked first and took a deep breath. He said, "That was new, and I liked it."

Olivia simply nodded yes in agreement.

Chuck mentioned it was close to supper time and asked,

"Is there a good restaurant nearby, Harry?"

"To be honest, Chuck, I don't know."

They were looking around the immediate area for any signs of a restaurant when out of the blue, a bright aluminum plane made a low pass over Prescott and directly over the parking lot where they were standing. They looked up and waved, knowing instantly, the pilot and the plane. Harry grabbed Ollie's hand and they jumped in the car, heading back to the field. Chuck and Vicky were close behind.

By the time they got to the field, *Ginny's Gin* had touched down and was taxiing on its way to a parking area. The tower had given him instructions to taxi to the far end of the tarmac. A ground crew was there waiting to guide him in. Harry and the others drove to the hangar and greeted Liz and Jim as they exited the plane.

Jim told the ground crew to refuel and service the engines with a new oil and filters. He handed the key to the Crew Chief who told him, "I would be more than happy to care for this baby, sir. I did some work for Emelia when I was a kid. That was an honor, and now to work on the same plane again. You don't know how happy you've made me, landing here."

"Well, I'm glad I've done that for you. I get the same response no matter where I land. It's great to hear that from people that still appreciate the old birds."

They left the field and went back into the city, to a restaurant Jim had spotted from the air.

Chuck asked, "How did you know this place was here, Colonel?"

"I had to make an emergency landing several years ago and Prescott was the only field for several hundred miles around. I was flying a Comanche back then, trying to make it to Omaha. I landed just in time. She was ready to pop a piston. My oil pressure had gone to near zero and I prayed she would hold together long enough to touch down.

This restaurant was here then, but it looked a lot different. Let's go inside and see what's changed. Jim was amazed how the décor and theme of the place was as he remembered it so many years ago. A short, stout woman came up to him and said, "I know you, don't I?"

"Well, I don't know, mam. How would you know me?"

"You are Jim Perry, the pilot that brought that Comanche in a while back, smelling of oil smoke with streaks of oil on your cheeks and the backs of your hands. You don't remember me, do you?"

"I'm working on it, mam. I remember walking in and asking a lovely lady if I could …use the …washroom. Was that you?" Jim asked.

"Yes, it was." She looked at Liz and asked,

"Is this your man?"

"He sure is."

"Don't give him up, he's a keeper. He spent a lot of time here helping me out with different things that needed fixin'. I think I kept him from making it home on time for Christmas, wasn't it, Jim?"

"Yes, Evie. I remember, now. Your hospitality and generosity, your good nature about everything is what made me late. I didn't want to leave. But we fixed what needed fixing and then I had to go. I never thought I'd make it back here again." He turned to Harry and told him, "I'm glad you enrolled here, Harry. Now you can make a very good friend in Evie."

"Oh, Evie, this is my fiancé, Elizabeth Ackworth, and her son, Harry and his girl Olivia. This is my best friend from our days in the B-52, Chuck Gamer and his wife Victoria. Folks, this is my long lost friend Evie Noland. Awful glad I landed in Prescott, Evie."

"So am I, Jim. So am I. Let me show you folks to a table."

In place of a picture window, was a mural of all the bombers that had ever landed at the Prescott field. Jim and Chuck stood a little too long admiring the picture.

"Fellas…Liz asked, "How about we place an order and enjoy the moment? We can discuss why we are here."

Olly and Harry looked at one another and smiled. Jim watched them in silence until it was time to say,

"Harry, I understand you want Olivia to stay here with you. Is that right?"

Harry nodded yes.

"And Olivia, you want to change your courses and join Harry in school, here…live with him? Is that right?"

Olly nodded yes.

"Alright, then, Olivia. You tell your story first."

A little embarrassed, she started to explain,

"You all know how we met, that night when I found Harry in my bed at home. Well, since then, I've had an uncomfortable feeling in my gut and no matter what I do, it won't go away. It's been six months, and though I may have dated other boys they haven't eliminated the discomfort. I wrote and told Harry how I feel…"

"You didn't tell me about the other guys." Harry said.

"So. You weren't around," she alerted him.

"Anyway, the pain only went away when I was with you, Harry. Ever since I wrote you, and then you wrote back on that lovely paper, in handwriting…I haven't been sleeping well. I talked to mom when I got home and told her, and here we are."

"OK, that sounds like a love-sick story," Jim said, "completely non-sensical. Isn't love grand? Now, Harry. It's your turn."

Harry looked around at everyone's faces and then stopped at Ollie. "I won't make it a dissertation in loneliness or a pain that won't go away. Simply put, I love her. I love you, Olivia Gamer."

"That took guts. In the company of your parents and for the first time, you've told us, you've told Olivia what is in your heart." Jim nodded saying it was all good.

Victoria looked at Olivia and nudged her arm, as if there was something she wanted her to say. Olivia looked at her mother and confessed, "I love him, mom. I can't find any other answer, than I love him." Looking at Harry she smiled and took his hand and said, "I love you, Harry Ackworth."

Chuck bowed his head and said, "Thank you, Lord."

Vicky asked, "What was that for?"

Chuck turned to Jim and they both said, "A safe landing."

C H A P T E R   1 5

Engagements

As the evening passed with good food, drink and conversation, Harry asked Jim and Betty,

"Did I hear you introduce my mother to Evie as your fiancé`? When did this happen? Mom?"

"Yesterday, at 10,000 feet," Jim told them.

Betty showed the ring with a big smile on her face.

"Well, I guess it's time. I don't think dad would mind. In fact, I think he would be very happy to see you happy again, mom. Congratulations." He got up to give his mother a kiss and to shake Jim's hand.

Liz then asked her son, "You've never spoken with me about those feelings you had. And I don't think you've spoken to Jim about them, either. Have you?"

"No. I saw the doctor at the school dispensary when the pain wouldn't go away. He explained it as, Love."

"And what did you write me as the cause?" Ollie asked.

"I made up some cock-a-maim scientific reason."

Ollie asked, "Do you remember what you wrote?" She pulled the letter out of her purse and read,

> *"It is a resultant anomaly acquired from contact with a member of the opposite sex. A non-physical interaction creating an unexplainable harmonic resonance that supersedes the natural positioning of the stars and the alignment of hormonal vibrations in the human body."*

Jim exclaimed, "Wow, Harry, that is a really, high pile of scientific crap you wrote there. Congratulations. The Nobel committee would love to hear that one."

"Oh, cut it out. No matter. It ended rightly. Didn't it, Ollie?"

Ollie looked at Harry and said, "Yes, it did."

Harry then asked Jim, "When are you two heading back to Rhode Island?"

"We don't have any plans. I would like to see the campus and what you're going to be doing; the kinds of planes they will have you in. I would like to meet the school president. I think I might know who he is."

"That is Major General Harold Reynolds, a nice guy. He asked me if my father was the same Donald Ackworth that climbed down into the bomb bay of a B-52 to release a bomb that got hung up. I told him what the general at the air base in Shreveport told me. He said he knew the General there and had heard that story. I told him, yes. That was my father."

Harry started to tear up, thinking of his father and the people who knew him so many years ago; of the brave act that saved a B-52 and its crew; of the DFC he was awarded.

"Dad, were you so ashamed of your actions that you couldn't tell me what you did?" Jim heard what Harry was saying and added,

"Men in war don't always tell of the things they do, Harry. Some of those things can't be relayed to people who have never lived them. As far as any medals are concerned, he didn't pursue them because he didn't think he did anything to earn them."

"But he risked his life!" Harry emphasized.

"Yes, he did, and that's what makes hero's, Harry. It's those people that step up at a time when they know the risk but take the chance anyway. They are the true heroes. Your father was a hero, but he didn't see it that way. Don't question what he did. He played the hand that was dealt him at the time, and he won."

Harry looked at Ollie and said, "I'm playing the hand being dealt to me now. Olivia Gamer, will you marry me?"

Ollie was shocked, that Harry would ask her in front of everyone, without a ring to present her. Liz and Vicky saw what Olivia was thinking. Liz removed the engagement ring Donald had given her when he asked her to marry him. She gave it to Harry to present to Olivia and he asked her again,

"Olivia Gamer, will you marry me?"

With some hesitation, "Oh, what do I do now? Take the ring? Say yes, to what; being tied down, in the middle of my schooling? I think I'll be happy. I don't know, but after all, I'll be with you, Harry, the source of my indigestion." She chuckled a little, then said,

"Yes! I will."

And Jim relayed, "and the crowd goes wild."

The three couples hugged one another and patted each other on the backs, passing 'Congratulations' between them.

They left the restaurant and made plans to meet in the morning.

At 07:00 AM, back in Prescott, they found a breakfast nook serving southwestern style omelets. Jim exclaimed of the coffee and the others agreed. Harry wasn't yet a coffee drinker but enjoyed the nook's homemade chocolate milk. When they were finished the women walked the streets and shops of Prescott, while the men went back to the airfield and walked the classrooms and hangars at the school.

Jim pointed out the different aircraft he had trained on, and Chuck mentioned how this aircraft might have this idiosyncrasy under the hood while the next would be a dream to work on. Harry took it all under advisement because he may have the opportunity to fly one of those questionable aircraft. He trusted Jim's and Chuck's advice because he knew some of their history in aviation.

After several hours the six met up again and Jim offered the ladies a ride in the Lockheed. *Ginny's Gin* was rolled out of the hangar and made ready for a flight around the Prescott area.

The ladies boarded, and Jim took them up to see where Harry and Olivia would be living, at least while they were in school. "It's a nice area for flying, pretty stable most of the year."

They returned after an hour of sightseeing. Jim offered a ride to Harry and Chuck, but Chuck said,

"Let her rest. You're going to need her on the trip back east."

They passed the evening relaxing with drinks under the stars of the Arizona sky. By midnight, Harry told them he had to get back to the dorm. He kissed Ollie goodnight and wished the others a goodnight's sleep. Jim, Betty, Chuck and Vicky, and Olivia stayed at the Hampton.

Harry left for the dorm telling them he had classes in the morning. "I will see you tomorrow noon. We will go to lunch." Everyone agreed and the night took over. Olivia wanted to go with Harry, but it wasn't permitted. They would see the school President in the afternoon about her enrollment and other arrangements for personal housing with Harry.

When afternoon came Harry took the group to the Earhart Dining Hall on campus. The buffet style menu was Jim's and Chuck's favorite kind of lunch; eat anything and everything you want or nothing at all.

"Men like food, don't they mom?" Ollie asked.

"Well, we know your father does. How about Jim or Harry, Betty. Do they make your food bill go up?" Vicky asked

"Every time I go shopping. Jim has only been living in the house for a few weeks, so I can't tell yet. But Harry is picky, some days he's ravenous other days he just picks at whatever is in the fridge."

Olivia was taking notes, hoping she would learn how to feed Harry this summer. She did not want to go back to Louisiana with her parents. She was hoping to transfer her credits from Carnegie Mellon to Embry-Riddle and take classes alongside Harry, her fiancé`.

The two kids went to the Bursar's office to present their case.

"Well, I can see she has outstanding grades in Math and Science, but in what field have you decided to enroll in?" the bursar asked.

Ollie didn't know for sure. "Engineering Physics looks good, and I do have an interest in the space sciences and the environmental sciences. More in the environmental than the Space, I think."

Harry looked over the requirements and wasn't happy that some of the courses were located at the Florida campus. He began calculating the time he would graduate from the Prescott campus and the time when Ollie would have to go to Florida to finish her Bachelors. "That would work," he thought.

"What would work," Ollie asked.

"I'll tell you about it later. If you want Engineering Sciences and you think you can handle it, go for it." Harry said.

"Now, about the housing…" Harry explained about their recent engagement and their desire to stay together. The Bursar told them the only co-ed housing they had was in the existing dorms, but the housing was males on the second floor and females on the first. That was the only way Ollie and Harry could live in the same house.

CHAPTER 16

Sky High Observations

George and Alexander paused for a moment in the making of the wings for Ollie and Harry. They looked down to watch which way Harry and Ollie were going to turn.

"Oh-oh," Alexander said. "This decision could make a change in color in somebody's wings."

"Hey, the Boss knows what he's doing. If they choose to live together, my bet is the Boss is going to sanction it. If they don't, my bet is he's going to sanction that, too. Look, here's a little bit of what's instore for the two of them."

Alexander explained to George what he knew of the future designed for Harry and Ollie. One, or both, were going to go through tough times, "But that is the natural course of being human. And I think the Boss is going to let this one play out. There's time before we have to finish their wings, so don't push the manufacturing."

"Whose wings are those? Are they part of this life's time- line?"

"Yeah, sorry to say. Nice person, a great life, will leave a good mark on many people. The ticket says the wings get delivered very soon. Now who put that on there? "Very Soon" is not a delivery date, George." Alex told him.

"I'll get that straightened out, but you know we are not in charge of delivery. That is left up to Michael and Gabe, so don't worry about it. Just concentrate on doing a good job. The Boss doesn't like presenting less than perfect wings."

"I know."

"And stop watching Harry and Olivia."

CHAPTER 17

A New Change

Harry and Ollie had decided to stay on campus and do the dorm thing to start out. She would live on the first floor with the other girls and Harry would live on the second floor with the other guys. Every morning they would pass each other on the way to class and exchange a kiss. Every evening, though it was a lot harder, they would do the same thing. Sometimes they would meet in the garden and study their material together, and sometimes they would get nothing done, spending time making up for lost time.

In the middle of the semester, Ollie's class was going to fly to the Florida campus for a week studying on a particular piece of equipment. The president had asked for volunteers to fly the students to Florida and Harry's hand went up. He wanted the time in type to put in his logbook. The plane chosen for the familiarity flight around campus was the Cessna Caravan. It was a work horse that could comfortably carry ten passengers. Its turbo prop engine would give him 180 knots, 1000 miles before refueling, and more of a challenge than the docile 152.

Chuck Wood would be the instructor taking Harry up for the check ride. Chuck sat in the right seat while Harry took the left. Weight was added in the cargo to simulate the weight the plane would have with passengers. Harry checked the books for the Caravan's limits and the recorded weight in the plane.

"Looks like we are in the green, Chuck, and with a full load of fuel."

"It's all yours, Captain." Chuck called him. "I like to think the man that fly's the plane is the captain. So that's what I'll call you." Chuck watched everything Harry did. From start up, run up, taxi, calling the tower, following their instructions, Harry was spot on. There was nothing for Chuck to note on his yellow pad.

They took to the air with such smoothness Chuck had to smile, and Harry immediately took to the airplane. He fell in love with its turbo-engine performance and overall performance.

"Oh, I could get used to flying this thing every day," Harry told him.

"Good to hear you say that young man. I am recommending you pilot this plane all the way to Florida. You won't have any passengers, just cargo, so it might get a bit boring. But, I think the school will let you take one person with you, of your choice. I think I know who that person will be, and I think they will allow it. So, you tell the General who you want in the right seat. And I'll back you up."

"You know it will be Olivia Gamer. She's my fiancée and having taken her up in the 152 a couple of times, she likes flying and she is a very quick study. I would be very comfortable having her in the right seat."

"Alright. Tell that to the General just like you told me."

When they landed, Harry went to the General's office and pleaded his case. The general scrutinized Harry's fly log and took a look at Ollie's books …. "And you think she would make a good right seat? Her ability might be good enough in a 152, Harry, but a Caravan? Does she even know what a turbo sounds like?"

Harry heard a racial slam, something he didn't expect from the general, but then he considered his age and experience behind him. The General then apologized, recognizing what he said was inappropriate.

"Sorry, Harry, that was uncalled for. Olivia's books look good, and I haven't got the nerve to tell you what you're doing right. Your books are perfect." The General reached into his desk and handed Harry a set of silver wings. Harry looked at them and asked,

"Sir?"

"I very rarely hand those wings out to my students. They have to be exceptional. Harry Ackworth, you are exceptional. I have no doubt that you can drive that Caravan all the way to Daytona."

"Thank you, General. I would be very proud to wear them."

As Harry was leaving, the General called him back for a moment. "The school is getting a Citation in the next couple of months and only select students will be chosen for training. I'm putting you on the list, Harry, if you want it."

Harry was stunned, that he was chosen to learn to fly the jet powered Citation. "Yes, sir. I would be honored."

"Good, now get out of here and say nothing about the Citation. The school won't release the information until the September semester begins. I don't want you to tell your fiancée, either, Harry."

"Yes, sir. I mean, no sir. I won't say a word."

Harry went back to his dorm and saw Ollie waiting for him. She asked in excitement, "What did he say? What did he say?"

"You get to ride with me in the right seat."

Ollie jumped up and down with excitement.

"But" Harry added. "It could be a bit boring. We will be flying cargo, no passengers."

"Just you and me, Harry? No one else, for 2000 miles?"

"Uh-huh."

"Fun," she said, feigning enthusiasm. "When do we leave?"

"Tomorrow. Everyone is to pack this evening. We take off at 0830 AM so we are at the field at 0730 AM. You and I will be the last plane in the group, watching the others."

"Well, at least we will have some time together," Ollie mused.

Harry drove to the field after supper to check out the Caravan. Ollie went along to see what she would be riding in for the next two days. Several other planes were lined up next to the Caravan; a Stationair HD, and a Skymaster at the end of the row.

"I know who's flying this beauty, Capt. Chuck Howe."

Harry was right. Capt. Howe told the group he was going to be leading the air-caravan to Daytona but didn't tell them what plane he would be flying.

Howe rounded up the students at 0730 the next morning. He told them, "Place your things in the Caravan on the end, then proceed to your designated bird. We will be in the air by 0830, so let's move it."

Harry's Caravan was off the runway at 0831 AM. He called the Capt. "Sorry I'm late Cap. Couldn't get off till 0831. I had traffic in front of me."

"Got to do better than that, Harry." He joked.

Knowing the Skymaster had the shorter distance rating than the Caravan, Howe calculated his fuel stops had to be just short of the big city airports. His first stop was the Abilene Regional Airport in Texas. The passengers got out to stretch their legs while the planes were being refueled. Before they were airborne all the vending machines in the terminal were empty.

"It looks like it's going to be a three day hop, Harry, and that's pushing it." Howe called back.

"Yes, I know, but we've got good weather for flying, Cap."

"Harry, can you carry anything but a positive attitude?" Howe asked.

Harry called back, "My father always told me to 'play the cards I'm dealt, until the day my wings are ready. Then I'll have no regrets.' That sounds like a positive attitude to me, Cap."

"Until your wings are ready, huh? Wow. That's looking forward, isn't it?"

"Yes," Harry thought of his father. "Yes, it is."

After a couple of hours, Harry called the captain, advising him the next best stop might be Pensacola, giving the credit to Ollie for figuring it out.

"You better keep her, Harry. Any woman who can guide a man to a landing zone like Pensacola is a keeper for sure."

"I'm working on it, Captain. I'm working on it," Harry told him, then he leaned over and gave Ollie a kiss.

The overnight in Pensacola was as comfortable as the overnight in Abilene, less than the beds in their dorms, but more than a sleeping bag under the fuselage. Captain Howe gathered the students after breakfast letting them know Daytona was their next stop. The temperature was like Prescott, just not as dry. They would have the opportunity to enjoy the Atlantic if they chose to but had to be in the classroom immediately following. There were a few groans at that requirement.

Airborne by 0830 AM, they landed in Daytona at 1300 PM. The planes were parked in front of the hangars so the A&P students could service them in their classrooms. After 8 days in class and two days on the beach everyone was looking forward to getting back in the air and back to Prescott.

CHAPTER 18

Wings Of Change

Capt. Howe had decided Harry needed a new level of responsibility. He gave him the Skymaster to fly back to Prescott, still with only the cargo and one passenger.

Harry looked at his boss and asked, "Are you sure this is the right step for me right now?"

"Harry, I'm tired of flying. I don't have anyone else I can give it to. As experienced as some of the other pilots are, I'm not sure I can trust it to them. You know how to handle that Caravan and it's the biggest of us. I've seen you take the Stationair for a ride and I've got nothing to complain about there. You know everything rudimentary in the cockpit. You've just got to watch twice as much. Olive…"

"Olivia, sir. Or you can call me Ollie," she interrupted.

"Ollie it is. She's going with you. I've seen her books and I have watched her hone her piloting skills. I have never had a student learn as quickly as she has. I figure the two of you can handle the Skymaster without any trouble. Now, the three planes are all within 10 knots of one another. Try staying in visual contact. If you lose sight of the guy in front of you, you're on your own. I'll be in the Stationair calling out our next fuel stop. Like before, you've got most of the cargo, so you'll be the last one up. And I'll see you at 13,500ft."

"Well, everybody has had breakfast and it's near 0800 AM," Harry said. "Time to board. I'll see you in…"

Capt. said, "I'll see when we get airborne. Happy flying. Keep an eye on him, Ollie."

"I will, sir."

"Nice going, girlfriend. Keep calling him sir. He appreciates it," Harry told her.

The pilots completed their walk around, ensuring everything was air worthy. The passengers were aboard, the cargo was loaded, and the tower gave each pilot clearance to enter the runway and hit the big blue. They joined up at 13,500 ft and cruised along at 165 knots.

Capt. Howe was aiming for Lake Charles, but it was a little farther than his gas tank would allow, so he settled for Lafayette. "Gonna fill it up with moonshine, Harry. That'll make them all run better." He told him.

"It should at least clean them out, Captain."

"You got that right."

Everyone disembarked and hit the rest rooms and the candy and soda machines. Harry bought a pack of cigarettes and a new lighter. Ollie asked him why. He said it was for the longer parts of the flying, when there's nothing to do but sit there. Ollie had recommendations for something to do. Harry looked at her and laughed. She blushed.

Back in the air, Harry got a weather report of a system brewing in the Caribbean and it was building up fast. Capt. Howe decided they would head north as far as they could; refuel and get out again before the storm was on them. He found a strip in Amarillo. Radioing ahead, the field had the fuel for the three planes, and they weren't expecting any foul weather for at least 24 hours. That meant they could get in and out on time. Now they had to make it to Amarillo in the next 4 hours.

Capt. Howe listened to the weather report change every hour. He instructed Harry and Bill Regents to pick up the same station.

Bill Regents was flying the Caravan. The three kept constant communications between them. Capt. Howe asked,

"How are you doing back there, Ollie? Is Harry giving you enough to do?"

"I'm doing fine, Captain. I kind of like this Skymaster. It's neat being the eyes and ears for Harry."

"That's what happens, dear, when you find the right partner."

"I guess you're right, sir," she said, looking at Harry. He turned and smiled back, then pointed to the south.

"That looks like clouds building."

"Harry!" Ollie pointed out, "We're at least 500 miles from the gulf. They can't bother us up here."

"I hope not, deary, but I'm no fan of outer winds and they can reach a long way. It'll all depend on how fast it builds up and how intense it gets. If we don't beat it out of Amarillo, we may be staying the night again."

"I wouldn't mind, Harry," Ollie shied.

"There are people watching, dear."

"Yeah, I know." And she slumped back in her seat.

They made Amarillo at 1800 hrs. and killed no time filling up. By 1850 hrs. they were back in the air and watching the skies. Turbulence met them west of Tucumcari. As they crossed the high plateau, the Skymaster's rear engine quit, and she began descending. Harry immediately called the captain.

"Move all your power to the front, Harry, as soon as you can. You're going to be playing with your pedals so watch what she does. Try to bring her down as soon as you can. Tell Ollie to search out a nice flat place to land. I'll call Mayday and let them know your co-ordinates. Howe called Bill Regents in the Caravan, "Go on ahead and get the girls back to school. As soon as I know Harry and Ollie are safe, I'll follow along."

"Harry? Do you know where the emergency gear is stowed?"

"Got it, Cap."

"Okay, as soon as your down and safe I'm heading up to Prescott. Stay with the plane. We will be coming for you."

"Roger!" Harry replied. He looked at Ollie, who had a worried look on her face. "Don't worry honey. If this is the worst, we ever go through we've got it made. Do you see anyplace that looks nice and flat, I'm getting awfully close to the ground?"

Harry was going to run into the Sandi mountains if he didn't land soon. He found a flat plain just outside Sedillo. He lowered the flaps and the landing gear and began pulling back on the wheel hoping to flair gently onto the side of the mountain and not into it. Ollie pulled tight on her belt and gave Harry's an extra tug. She heard Harry yell,

"Hang on!" then felt the mountain scrape along the belly of the Skymaster. They heard the landing gear tear away when Ollie asked,

"What was that, Harry?"

"I think we lost our landing gear."

The nose of the plane began to dig into the New Mexico soil when they struck a rock, hard, bringing the tail section up and over the top of the cabin. They were now upside down and Harry could smell fuel leaking from the tanks. He cut away his belt and reached over to cut Ollie's. He saw her body had gone limp and she was unconscious. Kicking the door open, he grabbed the emergency kit, and ran around to Ollie's side. He cut her belt and caught her fall, then carried her away from the plane before it exploded.

Laying her down on the mountain soil, Harry tried to revive her, but in shock he saw his fiancé was dead. He could not believe it, and he began to cry bitterly. It was the radio call from Captain Howe that made him stop.

"Harry…Harry, are you alright? Are you down safe?"

"No, Captain. I'm watching the Skymaster burn, sitting next to Ollie's body. She's dead. My fiancé is dead."

Harry shut the radio off and sat waiting for rescue. He put his head down between his knees and wished it was him that perished, not Ollie.

A rescue helicopter from Kirtland Air Force Base was on the scene in 30 minutes. An emergency helicopter from San Antonito flew in with a fire team to extinguish the burning Skymaster. The Air Force Team took Ollie and Harry to the base.

Captain Howe flew to Prescott and met Bill Regents dropping the students off. He reported to the General what had happened.

"Stay here and mind the store, Charley. Call the girl's parents and let them know what happened. I'll call Harry's mother and tell her."

The General notified Kirtland he was on his way in to pick up Harry Ackworth. Arrangements would be made to pick up Ollie. Jim and Betty were called and made arrangements to fly right out to Prescott. Chuck and Victoria were notified and flew out to Prescott on the first available flight. It happened to be on Jim's Electra. He called Chuck and told him he would stop to pick them up. The flight to Prescott could only be a sullen one. They couldn't talk of the accident. They didn't know anything just yet.

Jim was silent, keeping a secret to himself. He had gone through the same kind of incident Harry was now going through. Not long after he joined the Air Force, before he met Chuck, he too was involved in a plane crash. The first plane he owned, before he married Barbara Murray, had just left the shop from servicing. Jim and Barbara were traveling back to Vegas after their honeymoon on the east coast. At 12,000 ft the engine exploded. Both Jim and his new bride were covered in oil and Jim couldn't see where he was or where he was going. Disoriented, the plane began descending too quickly. They were over Wyoming trying to make it over the Rockies when it all happened. They hit the eastern slope of Mt. Chevo and the Piper Comanche began to burn. Jim got his wife out of the plane but found she had broken her neck when the plane impacted a rock under the thin soil.

Liz saw him Jim going back in time, and she saw the tear rolling down his cheek. "Jim, what's wrong, hon?"

"I didn't tell you before, but I went through what Harry's going though now." He began to relate the story of his early life before Liz, before the Air Force.

"I think now and again of what your husband told Harry when they spent time together."

"What was that Dear?"

"Harry told me his father always said, "You've got to play the hand you're dealt, and you've got to play fairly and honestly, until the time your wings are done…" or something like that." And I wonder why my wings aren't done yet. For all the stuff I've lived through. It makes me wonder what God still has for me to do."

George told them, "The idea of the wings being made ready for us sounds nice, but I never expected one of the kid's wings would be ready so soon…and not Ollie's." Vicky hugged her husband and echoed his sentiment.

"I can only think that Barbara's wings were ready, just as your husband's wings were ready for him. For whatever reason, our wings aren't ready yet."

Liz looked out the window thanking God Harry's wings weren't ready yet. "I'm sorry, Jim, about Barbara, and Chuck, Vicky…I'm so sorry about Ollie."

When they landed in Prescott the runway lights guided them onto a darkened field. Jim parked the plane and had the tower call a taxi for them. One light in the tower kept the controller awake to wait for the Electra. They were met by the General who drove them to a hangar, where they found Harry crying, sitting by Ollie's body, waiting for transport to the nearest funeral home. Chuck and Vicky were left alone with their daughter while Harry went outside to explain to Jim and his mother what happened.

He pulled out a cigarette and had a hard time looking his mother in the eye. He avoided contact to avoid the tears he knew would follow. He drew puff after puff until the cigarette was gone. Looking into Jim's eyes he nervously began telling him what happened. Between the tears he pounded his legs, waved his arms about, and blamed himself for the mistakes he must have made.

Jim grabbed the boy, though he was 24 years old, and an experienced pilot. "Stop, Harry. Stop!" He yelled. "There's no way to know what went wrong. An engine can blow itself up anytime, even two engines. I know!" He confessed.

"It happened to me, long before you were born. The same thing that happened to you and Ollie."

"You're just saying that to make me feel better."

"I wouldn't tell you that to make you feel better, son. I just never told anyone before. I feel that pain again. The same pain you're feeling now. But cry all you can, everything you have, let it out. It's the only way you'll be able to go on."

"Go on? Without Ollie? I don't know if I can. She brought out the best in me no matter what we did. And still, there was so much more we could have done, together. Now…" He turned to his mother,

"Mom? What did you do when dad died? Did you find it this hard?"

"Harder, son. Don't forget, we were in the middle of raising you. Your father and I weren't through with you. That was the last thing he told me when he died…he wasn't through with you. Then he told me he loved me and closed his eyes."

She clutched her son to her breast and said, "Harder, son. Squeeze harder."

Chuck and Vicky came out after telling the mortician to go and get her ready. They would have her body shipped to Shreveport for services and burial in the family plot.

Jim offered the Electra to transport Chuck, Vicky, and Ollie to the family home. Liz and Harry had decided to drive the Old's to Shreveport. His mother thought it was good way to talk to her son again. They made it an easy trip staying on I-10 and I-20 all the way into Shreveport.

Ollie's funeral drew friends from all across the country. Some of her friends had left school from as far away as England and Japan. Chuck's buddies from the Air Force dropped in and paid their respects.

Harry picked the first rose from the casket and held close to his chest. He waited on the side until all the roses were gone and all the mourners had left. He and Chuck stood by the grave waiting. They watched the workers lower Ollie's casket into the ground. Chuck told Harry,

"I don't blame you, son, not for any of this. We can only control what we do in life. We can't control death." Then he walked away leaving Harry alone.

Harry stared intently, perspiring heavily in the afternoon sun. His legs began to shake, and he reached for the headstone to steady himself. Cupping the rose between his hands he crushed it, and tossed it into the grave saying,

"Until my wings are done, sweetheart."

He walked away and rode back to the house with the family in the funeral car. Harry sat by the pool for a long time staring at the water. He had a beer and a cigarette just as he did that first night, he met Ollie. Then he went into the pool, and submerged himself, trying to wash the sadness away, wishing Ollie could be in the pool with him. Jim came out to the patio, saw Harry in the pool and jumped in with him, fully dressed.

When they came up for air, they stared at one another, and Harry asked, "Really, Jim, with your clothes on?" They laughed at one another, eventually crying in a deep hug. They left the pool and sat at the table. Chuck came out with three beers and joined them. Jim relayed to Harry the incident he had experienced at Harry's age, then grabbed one of Harry's cigarettes.

"Nice lighter," he told Harry. It was the lighter Ollie had given him. Harry looked at Jim and shook his head. "I don't want to believe she's gone."

"We know, son. Give it time. The pain will go away. It's the memories we keep that help us to go on."

Chuck started telling stories of Ollie growing up and how she did this and did that and almost this, and anything she wanted to. He thought he and Vicky might have given Ollie too much independence.

"No, not too much," Harry said. "But I wish we had the chance to experience each other's deep love." He looked at Chuck and said, "Your daughter is truly an angel with the purest of white in her wings. Thank you for giving me the chance to know, to love, a real angel, here on earth."

"Thank you, Harry. Your words mean an awful lot."

Harry got up and told Jim and Chuck, "I'm driving back to Prescott. Ollie would have wanted me to stay in school. Her enthusiasm for flying was growing more and more every day, every time I took her up. Going back, is the only way to honor her memory."

"Aren't you going to say goodbye to your mother and the others?"

"I think mom and I said all we had to say on our drive. The others…maybe they'll understand. Please convey my love and gratitude to Victoria. Thank her very much for her advice."

The three hugged and shook hands and Harry got into the Old's and drove back to Prescott.

CHAPTER 19

New Life Study

Three days later Harry pulled onto the base and walked over to the General's office. The General saw him walk in and stood up from his desk.

"You could have taken more time, Harry, if you needed it."

"No, sir. Ollie would have wanted me to keep going. This is the only way to hold onto her love and memory, by getting back in the classroom and the cockpit."

"Alright, Harry. Your class is two weeks ahead of you. There'll be some makeup to do if you want to graduate with them. Welcome back. Captain Howe will be glad to see you."

Before he left the office Harry turned and asked,

"Have any findings come back from the NTSB, sir?"

"Not yet, Harry. The damage was extensive. It's going to take a while. I'll let you know."

Harry went back to his classes and wasted no time picking up where things left off. He made one change, requesting a different dorm. It was difficult for him to walk past the room Ollie lived in. He was given a dorm closer to the field.

Captain Howe welcomed Harry with a hug and asked if he was ready to fly again. Harry told him,

"Ready or not, let's make it happen." Harry said. Then Howe took him to a different hangar. Opening the doors Harry saw a brand new Citation parked, awaiting inspection.

"She looks brand new, cap'n." Harry's eyes grew wide and sparkled at the white beauty.

"She only has ten hours on her, Harry, came straight from the factory. The students will be all over it, inside and out, before any of them ever get a ride. General Reynolds wanted me to tell you, Harry… you're being given the privilege of naming her, if you want to."

"Yes, I will. But I want to go through her with a fine tooth comb; learn every system and sub system, every nut and bolt, what they do and where they belong. And after I learn how she fly's then maybe she'll earn the name."

"Fair enough, Harry. I have your books; the manuals are in the plane. Study as long and as hard as you need to. You have some make-up to do, but something tells me you're going to graduate with your class."

Harry studied everything he could find on a jet engine, from the opening nacelle to the exhaust. And not only how the engine is built, but how it operates and what is supposed to happen and not supposed to happen when it is in operation, both at idle and full throttle.

He knew how the airframe was assembled, where it was assembled, and the materials used in the manufacture of each part. Harry consumed the Citation, on the ground and especially in flight. His instructors cautioned him about not thinking it was a fighter aircraft. But Harry knew the Citation was too big for that kind of flying. It was a commercial passenger carrier and nothing more, although it could be converted to carry cargo. He loved the jet and thought again about the privilege he was given.

Graduating at the top of his class, when the ceremony had ended and the class had gone, Harry asked the General and Captain Howe to accompany him to the Citation's hangar. He wanted them to witness the pleasure he took in naming the plane. Harry took a felt-tip marker and in his best script wrote on the side of the plane, *Ollie's Wings.* Howe and the General approved. The General saying, "Just like the WWII bombers. I like it, Harry."

Following graduation, Harry drove the Oldsmobile home to Rhode Island. The Old's was running well but Harry had concerns it might quit on him in unfriendly territory. He would rise early, drive all day, and find all-night rest stops to rest and get some sleep. The full bench seat was comfortable enough for a couple of hours. When he reached Rhode Island, he found a motorboat parked in the driveway and a brand new Dodge Ram pickup next to it. He beeped his horn to let his mother know her son was home. Liz came running out with Jim right behind. She gave him a big hug and a kiss and ushered him in. Jim shook his hand and said, "Welcome home, Harry."

"Mom, I'm home for a while, at least until I find a job."

In the house she offered him a cool drink and a sandwich, both he welcomed. Jim came out with a pile of mail, most of which had return addresses from the different aircraft manufacturers. They were filled with incentive bonuses and stipends to work for Boeing, MacDonald-Douglas, Aerospatiale, Airbus, Bombardier, even Cessna and Beechcraft reached out with offers to grab this aeronautical phenom. He was flattered by all the offers and saw his dreams of making a difference in the field of aviation coming true. But he didn't know where to turn. It felt like he was back in high school going through catalog after catalog of colleges and universities.

In the pile of offers, Harry found a brochure from the US Air Force. "Where did that come from?" Then he looked at Jim.

"Did this one come from you, Jim?" Harry held up the Air Force brochure.

"Yes, it did. With your level of education and flight experience, the certification on a Citation jet, you won't need a recommendation from a Senator or Congressman to attend the Air Force Academy. And dollars to donuts, you could probably ace every course and certainly come out an officer. From there, it's your choice as to what you want to fly." Jim's dissertation on the Air Force made an impact and Jim could see it.

Harry told his mother he would make an appointment to see the local recruiter. Jim told him,

"I've been out a few years and I know things have changed. The greatest change, I think, has been to the planes. They fly faster and higher than ever before. The pilots have to match the planes capabilities and that can be difficult but very rewarding."

"Okay, Jim. Your pitch got me to make an appointment. I don't need anymore. I have, after all, flown and am certified on a Citation. My resume` should say something. Do you want to go down with me when I sit and listen to the recruiter give me his pitch?"

"Yes, I would like that. Thank you."

The day came for Harry's appointment with the Air Force recruiter. Jim showed off his new pickup truck on the way down.

"It does ride nice," Harry told him, and Jim went on and on until they got out of the truck. Harry was about to say,

"I'll trade the Old's for a pickup," but stopped short of actually saying it. They walked into the recruiter's office and listened to his pitch. After an hour, Harry walked out with an application to the Academy.

CHAPTER 20

Heavenly Observation

George and Alex watched as Harry and Jim left the recruiter.
"That was too bad about his fiancé. I didn't expect that change to occur in his life, not so soon. I guess we can hold off on his wings, Alex?"

"Yeah, for a while. The model we had did come in handy for Ollie though. Those wings fit her just right."

"So, what do you suppose Harry is going to do now?" George asked his compatriot.

"I'm betting he joins the Air Force and puts his piloting skills to the best use possible." Alex surmises.

"Flying?" George asks.

"Of course, and probably for a very long time," Alex tells him.

"You know something I don't know, don't you Alex?"

Alex turns his head away and says, "My lips are sealed."

"I guess Ollie will have to wait to see him again, huh?"

"Yeah. I guess so," Alex smiled.

"You know we cannot interfere in their lives, Alex. What are you saying?" George states.

"I'm not saying anything, George. Just watch and keep building those wings. There are souls waiting for them."

CHAPTER 21

Into the Atmosphere

Harry entered the Air Force Academy that fall and surprised all the instructors with his knowledge of the rudiments of flying, the lift properties of airfoils and wings, and architecture of building a strong, yet lightweight, airframe. He dove into the physiology and psychology, the mental stresses on the human body in flight. Harry's explanations of the course material were impressive, and his professors were amazed at his grasp of every subject and abilities placed into practice.

Again, Harry graduated at the top of his class, but this time he was wearing the uniform of an Air Force Officer. He attended fighter pilot school at Shepherd Air Force Base in Texas. His kill score was becoming legendary.

After graduation, Harry requested to be stationed overseas. His group was sent to Qatar and the Al Udeid Air Base. The US had a group of F-15 Strike Eagles and F-16 Fighting Falcons. Two F-22 Raptors stood by to lend a hand if needed.

On a peace keeping mission patrolling the Saudi Coast, Harry and his group came across a group of Iranian Mig-29s out of their designated area. Warned to return to their own airspace they defied the request and fired on the American fighters. The dog fight lasted a hot 28 minutes with one American fighter lost, pilot recovered in the water, and three Mig-29 KIA's. After one year in Qatar Harry made ACE with 8 kills and was returned to the US. He wasn't yet 30 years old and was continuing to miss Ollie.

Harry's next duty station was Barksdale Air Force Base in Shreveport, Louisiana. It was one of the few remaining SAC bases with two groups of B-52 stationed there. He could feel Ollie's presence. Her grave wasn't far away, and her mother and father lived just off base. He purchased a lease on a house in Princeton, north of the airfield. The area was quiet, the road was a dead end. It wasn't a big house, so he didn't have a great deal to add to it. When he went into town to look for furniture he might want, he made it a point to stop in and see Chuck and Victoria.

He had traded the Olds for a new BMW. He was also wearing his pilot's uniform when he knocked on the door. An old face behind a new mustache greeted Chuck when he opened the door. Stunned, Chuck went up and down the uniform, stopping at the eagle on the collar and then the name on the breast, 'Ackworth'.

"Are you the same fella that was here 8 years ago to help bury my daughter Olivia?"

"I am, sir. And I've come to honor your daughter's name by paying a visit to the two most influential people in my life."

"Oh, bullshit!" Chuck grabbed hold of Harry and gave him an enormous hug. "It is so good to see you, Harry. You look like you've made a few strides in your life. A Colonel! Wow!"

"Vicky, come see who came to pay us a visit."

Harry saw a wheelchair come around the corner from the kitchen and immediately felt some discomfort. Vicky said,

"Don't fret the chair, Harry, or feel sorry for me. Things begin to fall apart when you get our age. The chair makes it a lot easier getting around. I may not drive anymore, but that's what I have Chuck for, anyway. Come in, sit down, or would you rather go out by the pool?"

"The pool, if you don't mind. I enjoyed some brief but profound memories there," he told them. Harry pushed Vicky out to the pool while Chuck brought out three beers and a pack of cigarettes. Harry laughed. "It's kind of you to remember the important things that happened here."

They sat and talked for almost three hours. Vicky offering snacks and a supper, if Harry wanted to stay.

"I can't; thank you. I have an all-night flight and I don't want to have to use the facilities on the plane if I can avoid it. You know what it's like up there, Chuck."

"Yes, I remember. When did you get stationed here?"

"Just a month ago. I stayed on base while I looked for a place of my own. I just signed a lease on a home in Princeton, North of the base. It's on a dead-end road, for now. It looks like a place that could easily be developed. The wooded section behind the house easily invites me to walk through and clear my head when I need to." Harry paused, not sure how to say what he wanted to tell them.

"I can feel Ollie's presence, you know. As soon as I got into town something came over me. I wasn't dizzy or disoriented. I just felt her presence, almost as if... if I turned around, I would see her there." Harry took a cigarette from his pocket and lit it. Then he stopped, and he felt someone touch his hand. "There it is again. Ollie, stop playing with me!" He shouted. "I can't take you being gone, isn't that enough?"

Chuck and Vicky looked at Harry and told him,

"It's okay, Harry. She does the same thing with us."

"She does? Why? Doesn't she know we hurt enough?"

"No, son. She doesn't. Vicky had a conversation with Olivia the other night. I didn't know what to say, watching them talking together. Then she said "The angels are making your wings, mom. We'll be together soon."

"I almost lost my mind that night, here my dead daughter is telling my wife she's leaving soon, going to get her wings?" Chuck was shaking telling Harry the story.

"It's a crazy thing, Harry, but people around here say that happens all the time. It's as if their dead relatives don't want to leave. We had to ask the church for help. They said they knew about the visitations and there was nothing they could do about them. 'Accept it,' they said. 'It won't last long.'

"How long does it last," I asked. They told me,

"Until their wings are done."

Harry stood up, stunned, recognizing that statement.

"Until my wings are done. Something my father used to say." He fell into a silence not ready to believe Ollie was playing with him because her wings weren't ready. "Ridiculous," he told himself, aloud.

"That's what we said, Harry, but once we understood, Olivia only comes around, now, when she feels, senses, oh, I don't know the word. When we want to remember her most. You know, a memory of her that comes back, and we can't let it go… then she comes to offer comfort."

"She told us her wings are almost complete. The only thing left…" Vicky paused.

"Tell him, Victoria."

"Tell me what?" Harry pushed.

Chuck spoke up. "Olivia said she will leave us alone when you have a new friend, and then she will leave you alone."

"That's not fair for her to do that. She should be gone by now, give us time to be without her in our lives."

"Harry, it's been 6 years. We had no idea that you…"

"That I was still carrying a torch for her? Yeah, I'm still waiting for her to come back." Harry confessed. "The whole thing is driving me nuts."

The doorbell rang and Chuck got up to answer it.

"I think it's Elouise, Vicky." Vicky looked at Harry and told him,

"Elouise is my therapist. She comes once a week and helps me with my exercises. It gives Chuck a break and I get to talk to a woman. Sit and watch her, she's very good. You'll like her, Harry."

Harry saw the therapist walk in and made an excuse to go out to the patio. He grabbed another beer and took his shoes off to dangle his feet in the pool. Reaching for another cigarette he paused before lighting it. An unnerving feeling invaded Harry's sense of wanting to be alone. He turned around and saw no one, but he could feel 'eyes' were watching him. Flippantly, he said, "Ollie, is that you?" And looking to his left he saw Ollie sitting beside him on the edge of the pool.

"You need a new friend, Harry," she spoke.

"What? What did you say?" he responded in surprise.

"It's been long enough, my love. You've gone and done so much, even dangerous things, but you've done them all alone."

Harry stared at the vision sitting beside him.

"I can't talk to you, Ollie. You're dead, you can't hear me, and I can't see you."

"That's what most people want to believe, Harry. Someone dies and they think that person is gone forever… *'You'll always be in my heart'*, they say to themselves. That can be true, Harry my love, but we hear you. We really do. It's only those we chose to visit we allowed them to see and hear us."

Harry composed himself and, *'went along with the game.'* "Dad said when your wings are ready, you're gone."

"Partly true. Your dad has his wings. I saw him."

"You saw my father?" he said, alarmed.

"Yeah. He's a good looking man, Harry. But yeah, and he's doing fine. You don't have to worry about him."

"Can I see him?" Harry asked.

"I can't tell you anything about that. I don't know. That decision is not mine." Ollie toyed with him and grabbed the cigarette. He felt her take it from him. She spoke again,

"You see me, you feel me, here, because you won't let me go. And you have to let me go, Harry. I was allowed to come back to tell you that a new friend is nearby and that you should pay attention to that, to her, like you did to me."

"I don't know if I can, Ollie. I miss you so much."

"I know, Harry, but I can't miss you. It doesn't work that way here. All we can do is care, not feel, like we did, like I did, when we were together. Ollie paused and touched Harry on the shoulder. He froze and listened,

"What now?" he asked.

"There's a pretty gal in the parlor with my mother. She is to take my place, Harry. It has been written and promised for many years to come."

"I suppose you're going to get jealous."

"Jealousy is not something we do up here, Harry. In fact, we encourage the pairing of new partners by subtly suggesting their next move."

"I don't think that was a subtle suggestion on your part. It sounded quite direct."

"Yes, my fault, that's one of the reasons I came to you today, at my folk's place. I can come here and talk to my mother. My father doesn't believe as she does, so he thinks mom is losing her mind talking to me. But mom's wings are almost done, she'll be leaving him shortly."

"What's your father going to do, all alone?"

"He'll be taken care of, Harry, don't worry. Higher powers prevail."

Ollie stood up and walked to the window, watching her mother and the therapist. Vicky turned her head and smiled at her daughter's presence, talking to Harry. The therapist also acknowledged Ollie standing in the window. Harry stood, shaking his head watching the two women in the house waving at someone he's talking to but shouldn't be seeing. He didn't know if he was lucid or confused, in a false reality, or was this something real?

"Don't be a stranger, Harry," Ollie told him. "Start a new ball rolling by going in and saying hello. That's the only way I'm going to get out of here. When you have someone that can make you happy again, then I am free to go where I belong. I can take mother with me. My dad's wings aren't ready yet."

"Why are you telling me all this, Ollie? No one is supposed to know their future. I suppose you want to tell me when my wings will be finished." Harry asked.

"No, Harry. I don't know that. That would be against the rules, and an angel can get thrown into hell for that. Besides, I am not allowed to know that information. I will tell you the angels stopped making your wings. Orders from above."

"Oh, come on, Ollie. I can see you haven't lost your sense of humor."

"Oh, no. We get to keep that. We need it when we come here. Now get up, Harry, and go introduce yourself to Elouise, or I'm going to push you into the pool."

"Yeah, sure. You can't push me," Harry told her.

Just then he felt a heavy hand on his chest push him backwards into the pool. Harry yelled in the suddenness, and fell in, fully dressed.

Vicky and Elouise saw Harry fall back into the pool, and Elouise ran from the house and dove in after Harry, fully clothed.

"Don't fight me. Just relax." She told him, bringing him onto the edge of the pool where Chuck helped pull him out. Harry looked around wanting to yell out at Ollie. He shook his fist and began "Why you…" and suddenly stopped. Like a slap in the face, he turned around and came to be standing nose to nose with Elouise's beauty.

"Ollie was right. You are beautiful." At that he felt Ollie disappear.

During their visual exchange, Vicky had gone into the house to get towels for the two.

"How did you fall in?" she asked. "I saw you standing there, looking like you were coming into the house, then suddenly you're in the pool."

"You wouldn't believe me if I told you." Harry said, star struck.

Elouise looked at Vicky and Chuck. The three said together, "Olivia!"

"Oh. So, you know about her, too."

Vicky asked Harry, "Give me your uniform Harry, I'll dry it for you."

Embarrassed, Harry turned away from Elouise. She turned her back allowing him to wrap himself in the towel. He handed his uniform to Vicky. "Thank you, Vicky."

"It'll be about 30 minutes, Harry."

They sat at the table and Chuck brought out some beers.

"Everybody that's come to this house knows Olivia. She's made her appearance to me, and like you, I didn't believe it at first. A patient I see on the north side of the airbase has had the same thing happen to her. She lost a son a while back, her husband past several years ago. Her son comes back and entertains her occasionally, but she thinks his next visit will be to take her home with him. Those that believe, are visited by their loved ones."

"Do you believe, Elouise?"

"Oh, yes. I've had no visitations by past relatives, but I have seen Ollie and have heard from many people in my practice not to believe, and I don't have any relatives in this area. I'm from Attleboro, Massachusetts." Elouise told him.

"What are you doing down here?" Harry asked, and the conversation went on until it was time for Harry to leave. Vicky came out and handed Him a dry uniform.

"I'm sorry, Elouise. I don't mean to be rude and end a perfectly wonderful conversation, but I must get back to the base. I'm on duty tonight and have to get my plane in the air."

Harry stumbled trying to get his uniform on, watching Elouise all the while.

"It was very nice to meet you, Elouise. Vicky, Chuck. Can I take a rain check on that supper? Maybe you can invite Elouise to the next one?"

"I can do that for you, Harry," Vicky told him.

"Nice. Okay. I've got to go. Nice time, Elouise, bye."

Harry was gone and on the road in a flash, leaving Elouise, Vicky and Chuck laughing. Elouise turned to Vicky and asked,

"He's the one that dated your daughter?"

"Yes, he is," Chuck admitted. "I think he found you very personable, very interesting, and also very beautiful. You are you know." Chuck told her.

"Well, thank you, Mr. Gamer."

Elouise agreed to attend a supper at Vicky and Chuck's home.

"I hope he's able to come. I find him interesting and

unassuming. Would you care to tell me something about him so I can prepare myself?"

Chuck and Vicky let out a few secrets about Harry.

"Harry is a dedicated individual no matter what he does. When he gets involved in something, it's all the way. He might take his time deciding, but it is usually the right decision. About flying for instance, Harry went to school at Embry-Riddle in Daytona. He learned to fly; take planes apart and put them back together again, and they fly better than before. He attended their campus in Prescott, Arizona and furthered his understanding in aviation and planes and the science of flying. Chuck told Elouise, "6 years ago, after burying my daughter, he attended the Air Force Academy, learned to fly fighters, and became an Ace with 8 kills over Afghanistan and Iran, Saudi Arabia. He was recently reassigned here at Barksdale to fly B-52's. Those are bombers, and they carry nuclear weapons. They go up and stay aloft for 24 hours, longer if needed, and they patrol a designated area with 3 or 4 other bombers in other areas around the globe. It is dangerous work, but it is necessary work."

"I see," Elouise declared with inquisitive interest. "I think I would very much like to sit down and personally meet this Colonel Harry Ackworth. He sounds like he could be a lot of fun."

"Do you suppose he might be willing to tell me about the accident and how your daughter died? I don't want to impose on your loss but knowing more about Harry is better than not knowing enough."

Chuck told Elouise, "We can tell you only what the school told us, what the NTSB findings were. Harry is the only one that knows what happened up there."

"Yes, of course. Alright then. I'll leave it alone and let Harry tell me, when he's ready."

"Well, I guess this session is over. Same time next week, Ellie?" Vicky suddenly realized the faux pau she just stepped in, the similarity of 'Ollie' and 'Ellie'. "Oh, my."

"I recognized it the first time you told me about your daughter. I purposely didn't use Ellie when introducing myself to Harry because of that. A man who carries a torch that long was truly in love." Elouise stopped to think a moment.

"Mrs. Gamer, Vicky, I'm not sure about this dinner thing with Harry. Perhaps it's not a good idea. Harry has a lot on his plate, and

I don't want to be the one to imbalance it. I'll say goodnight and see you next week."

"But Elouise…"

"Goodbye, Vicky, Chuck."

Elouise left wondering why she was feeling 'something in her gut' suddenly. "Ellie, Ollie," she wondered, our names are too close. Harry might want to do something about that."

"Stop the truck, Ellie." Said a voice somewhere in the cab.

"What? Who?" Ellie questioned.

"Stop the truck." Again, the voice insisted.

Ellie pulled over and gazed around the cab. "What are you doing, girl. You're the only one here."

"You're the only one alive here," the voice answered her.

"Ollie? Is that you? What are you trying to do to people, drive them crazy?" Ollie appeared, as a reflection in the truck's window. "Geez-is, Ollie! You scared the shit out of me."

"Sorry, Ellie, but this is serious business. I had that same 'feeling' in my gut when I first met Harry. He told me there was this 'sensation' he called it when we met. It's not a stomachache like Harry thought it was. He even went to the doctor for an explanation. The doctor told him it was 'Love', plain and simple, Love. I didn't put it there, the Boss did. Something about chemistry. But there's no need to go into that."

"But you can't tell me what to do with my life, who to love, who I might marry, what to eat, etcetera."

"No, we can't tell you what to eat, but that guy you've been seeing on and off has been seeing someone else, on and off. And I do mean ON and off. He's using you, Ellie. I will be surprised if he does not ask you for money."

"Jack wouldn't do that! He's a nice man."

"His picture is in the Post Office, Ellie."

"Now, you're toying with me, Ollie. Jack is not seeing someone else, and his picture is not in the Post Office. Shame on you for telling lies. You are never going to get your wings."

Ollie spread out her wings, big and white and gave Ellie a smirk. "Got 'em this morning, not that there is a morning or night for us."

"How did you get them?"

"Because you're here, now, Ellie, and I can go. I have to come back in a little while, though, to pick up my mother, and then again in a month to pick up my father. But you should think about Harry, Ellie. He's a great catch."

"I'm not fishing, Ollie," she hollered. Then Ollie was gone. Ellie sat senseless and quiet in the heat of the truck's cab, the windows rolled up.

A knock on her window made her jump. It was a police officer who had stopped to check on a vehicle parked on the side of the road.

"I watched you for almost 5 minutes before walking over," he said.

"Are you alright, miss? People driving by had reported seeing a vehicle on the side of the road. They thought the driver was slumped over. Are you sure you're alright?"

"Yes, oh yes. I'm fine. Thank you for stopping. I stopped to search for something in my bag," she told him.

"This is a busy road, mam. You have to keep moving. There is a rest stop just a mile up this road. You can pull up over there and search your bag."

"Okay, thank you, Officer. I'll do that." Ellie drove the mile down the road to the rest stop and got out of her car. The night was beginning to cool down the daytime temperatures. She walked around the car talking to herself, gesturing with her hands as if talking to someone else, as if talking to Ollie.

"How do you know I'm ready for him? How do you know Harry is ready for me? We both have careers we're working on." Elouise calmed down and got back into her car. She rolled down her windows and drove home.

CHAPTER 22

Dinner And Tomorrow

Ellie had a fitful night, tossing and turning. Ollie came in and came out, Harry made an appearance. There was just no sleep to be had. She got up as the sun hit her pillow.

"What's the use of staying in bed?"

It didn't take long for the morning sun to warm her room. Routinely, she began each day with a series of yoga exercises. Fully awake, she dressed for a run along the 12 mile Bayou. Ellie cherished the quiet of the early morning, when there were no other joggers. Cadillac Street dead-ended at her house, set in a grove of Japanese bark Maple and Sawtooth Oak. It was well cooled from the summer heat.

Back at the house, the coffee had finished brewing, so she jumped in the shower before having her first cup. Ollie's words kept repeating, over and over. Then she envisioned Harry, smiling at her at Vicky's house, staring at her, nose to nose, after pulling him from the pool. She got that feeling in her gut, again. Looking up, she closed her eyes and let the shower beat down on her face, trying to find an answer to all that was happening. She laid out a plan to first call Vicky and accept the invitation to dinner, with Harry in attendance. It was all set for the coming weekend.

Chuck called Harry and recommended he pick up Ellie for the informal dinner. Harry found the house on Cadillac Street. Ellie saw him coming up the drive and met him at the door. Struck again by her beauty, he shook his head, and smiled at his good fortune. She wondered, "Why are you shaking your head? Is something wrong?"

"No…it's like the Clapton song, I just heard on the radio, 'You look wonderful tonight.'"

"Oh, thank you, Harry. You look good, too. I wish I could think of a song that fit. I am very much looking forward to this evening," she told him.

Vicky served her delicious jambalaya. Harry picked up a bottle of red and a bottle of white wine, one for the dinner, one for dessert. Ellie commented,

"You choose your wines, well, Colonel Ackworth."

Harry laughed at her formality. "Just Harry will be fine, mam."

"And you can call me Ellie, or Elouise, nothing formal," she added with a smirk.

"Well, I'm glad that's out of the way. After our first meeting I wasn't sure how I was going to handle a second."

"I'm not that difficult to know, Harry." As they drove on Ellie remarked, "I have a strange feeling in my gut."

Harry stopped the car and asked, "Do you feel like you're going to throw up? Do it outside the car, please?"

Ellie looked at Harry who was already standing at her door, offering his hand to help her out. She took it and stood nose to nose with him, again. "We've been here before," he recalled.

"I thought you were going to throw up?"

"No, Harry. Not throw up…give up." She then kissed him fully and with a great deal of passion. Harry reciprocated with the same zeal, then heard the words, "Bye, Harry!" He pulled back and looked around, wondering who spoke.

Ellie heard, "He's all yours, now!" She looked up and said, "Thank you, Ollie."

Harry said in surprise, "You said, 'thank you, Ollie.' Why?"

"And I'll bet you heard something like, 'Bye Harry,' didn't you?"

"Yeah, how did you know?"

"I saw Ollie last night on my way home from Vicky's regular session. She told me she was going to pick up her mother shortly and then her father. She has her wings, Harry, and they are beautiful."

"I thought she had them already? It's been almost 7 years."

"She told me she had to wait until you were in the right place, with the right person, then she could leave."

"So, you are the right person?" He stopped to think,

saying to himself, "After that kiss, what's to think about? I don't have to think anymore, everybody is doing it for me."

"I can be the right person, Harry, if you want me to be. Will I take Ollie's place? No one will ever take Ollie's place. No one ever takes the place of the first lover in our lives, no matter how serious the second time around is. Just walking hand in hand can be a serious thing, Harry. If you want to start there, I'm okay with that."

Harry stared into Ellie's green eyes and told her,

"I don't know." Side stepping the issue, he offered,

"Let's go to dinner, Chuck and Vicky are waiting." When they arrived, they were smiling and holding hands.

The night moved on with the familiarity of a long friendship and more. Vicky and Chuck felt a new love growing between Elouise and Harry. Feeling the relationship was sanctioned and approved by Ollie, they were very happy Harry had found a new love. Vicky understood why Ollie kept coming around and knew she would be seeing less and less of her daughter as time went by.

Ellie and Harry were seen as a steady and regular couple everywhere in Shreveport. Harry introduced Ellie to the joy and exhilaration of flying, in everything from a single engine Piper Cub to a twin engine Cessna 310-B.

Ellie began taking flying lessons when Harry was on duty in the 52's. She would go up with the instructor and spend extra time studying the planes and the various characteristics of the different models. Her ability to take it all in surprised her instructors. She was a quick study, exact and correct in her tests, precise in her control of the wheel of any model. She received her Private Pilot's license and went on to get her night and instrument rating, Harry was proud that now he found a partner he could relate to, one that understood the pressures and pleasure of flying.

Harry was off duty for four days. He stopped at the small municipal airport that offered flying lessons at an introductory price. A Cessna 180 had just touched down and was rolling her way to the parking lot in front of the hangar. Harry spotted Ellie in the left seat and knew she had just flown solo.

Ellie saw Harry walking up to the plane and exited with excitement. "Did you see me? Did you see me? Oh, I have to thank you for introducing me to flying, honey. It's wonderful up there."

"I'm glad you like it, Elli, but don't be too exuberant about it. The weather has a lot to do with how you enjoy the flight. Bad weather is something you try to avoid because if you can't get above it or outrun it, you are stuck in it, and that place is unpleasant."

"I've got four days off. I was thinking we might get married and go off someplace private and quiet and idyllic."

He stopped, got down on one knee, and pulled a one carat diamond engagement ring from his pocket. Then he took Ellie's hand, and in front of all the people in the hangar and on the field, all those in the office he asked her,

"Elouise Haines, I never thought I would make it back from the edge of the abyss, but you reached out and put my feet on solid ground, with your sweetness, your caring, and your love. A man can't do better than that in life. I would like that the rest of my life. Will you marry me?"

"Harry Ackworth, a man like you, doesn't come around very often. Your brand of sensitivity, consideration, genuine caring for others, not to mention the love you've given me, has told me not to let you go. I don't want to. Yes, I will marry you."

Cheers and whoops and hollers arose up and down the field. A kid with a camera came by and shot a picture of Harry down on one knee. Then another in the middle of a kiss. Harry asked him,

"Hey kid, what your name?" he hollered back, "Jimmy Olson."

Harry laughed and told Ellie, "That's the same name as the cub reporter in the Superman comics."

Harry's 4 days were spent in the nearest Chapel, the best tavern, and a flight to Providence to catch up with his mother and Jim. Harry also wanted to take Ellie out for some top rated seafood.

Jim and Liz gave them the house for the night while they took the boat down to Warwick and the bungalow on the beach, a summer place the Ackworth family owned. Harry and Ellie made the most of their stay and joined Jim and Liz on the coast, down the channel to Newport. Harry saw that he wasn't going to get back to Barksdale on time for his 24hr shift in the -52. He called the base and explained his predicament.

"Harry," General Stowell asked, "are you playing hard and fast with the rules again? Just because you got married doesn't mean you get special privileges. I'll approve a weeks' extension. I'll write it up as an emergency…your balls were on fire. That will sit well with the staff. Have fun Harry. See you when you get back."

"Thank you, General." He told Ellie, "I get to stay a week. Any longer and I'll get court marshalled."

The four of them were enjoying the time together when Jim suggested they take the Electra and fly up to Brunswick, Maine.

"It used to be a Naval Air Station but now it's called Brunswick Landing, out of some realignment crap the government did to save money. I think they made it easier for our enemies to get into the country, but that's another story."

A cab took them into the center of town where they could walk through the history of one of Maine's oldest communities. They had dinner at an Irish Pub, walked down to a bakery and sampled Liz's favorite, a multi-layered chocolate cake. Harry spotted a gelato shop not far away and had to sample three and four of the most popular flavors. Jim walked into the 'Fume-adore', a cigar shop with the best of the best cigars. He found a bench away from the crowd and lit one up.

"Come and join me, Harry," Jim asked.

Harry looked at Ellie, and she said,

"Go ahead, but you won't be doing that in the house."

So, Jim and Harry sat and smoked their wonderful Panamanian/Honduran cigars and talked like the best friends Jim wanted them to be. Liz and Ellie walked down the main street stopping in front of this dress shop, that trinket store, talking like mother/daughter-in-law.

"Do you have any secrets about Harry I should know, Liz?" Ellie asked.

"He's very neat, orderly, not obsessive, but constant. He does like to dress up, when he has to. He is a very comfortably dressed man. He doesn't usually smoke, but he likes a cigarette with a beer. His father was like that."

"Tell me about Harry's father. Everything has happened so fast we really haven't had time to sit and talk."

"Donald was a worker, and a thinking man, a very kind and generous man. He loved me and he loved his son, but he did not spoil him. Don made sure Harry earned any reward he received, either in the house or in school, on the job, anywhere. And Don taught him so many things. Hunting and fishing, Don taught him how to catch a fish, clean it and cook and how to properly dispose for the.

"You bury them when you're camping. You don't toss them into the woods like trash," he would say. "You strive to leave as small a sign as possible when you camp. You don't want to tell people you were there." And Harry was a good student no matter what his father tried to teach him. After Don's long day and on weekends, he always made time to be with Harry or with me, but Harry first."

He tried to instill in Harry a sense of right and wrong, not letting society teach his son what society wanted. He knew Harry was going to run into situations where he had to make up his mind in a hurry, and deciding, 'is it what society wants, or is it truly a right or wrong situation.' He told Harry,

> *"Life doesn't have to be fair. You can control your life, but you can't control your dying. You play the hand life gives you. You play it fair, and you play it honest, until your wings are done."*

"That stuck with Harry and that's the way he lives his life, until his wings are done." Ellie told her what happened in Shreveport with Ollie, and the visits and signs Ollie was giving about getting her wings.

"It threw Harry for a loop," she told her. "He couldn't deal with the dead being a visual thing until he saw Ollie again. Now he knows there is always someone watching us, but they don't always tell us where they are."

"So now, you know as much about Harry and his father that you need to know. Anymore Ellie, and life won't be much fun. You need surprises. Just hope they are good ones."

Liz and Ellie walked back up to find the men had gone across the street to a local tavern. They were sitting outside enjoying a beer with their cigars.

"We are ready when you are," Ellie said.

"Yes, we were about to get up to find you," Jim said. "I would like to get back in the air before sundown."

The same cab driver brought them back to the air strip. He happened to park in sight of the Electra and commented to Jim,

"There's a fine looking airplane." The old cabby left his seat and walked to the fence to stare at the aluminum beauty. Jim didn't have to second guess the cabby's actions. Everyone got out and walked to the fence. The Electra was reflecting the bright red of the coming sundown and looked like an advertisement to a sale, all shined up for the public's taking. Jim asked,

"Do you know the Electra?" he asked.

"I used to know her inside and out. I was the mechanic, on this very base, and we kept a couple of recon ships in the air during the war. Two of those ships were Electra's."

"Would you like to see her?" Jim asked him.

"It would be a great pleasure to, but I don't have a lot of time."

"Come on, that's my plane. I'll give you a tour of your own memory."

Liz and Ellie smiled as Harry, Jim and the cabby made their way to the plane. Jim showed the old man inside the cockpit. He was surprised at all the modern radios that had replaced all the dials and switches or yesterday.

"This is an interesting difference," the old cabby told Jim. "I can see the need for the change, but it takes away from the nostalgia. Can I see her number?"

"Sure," Jim said to him, "But why?" Jim showed him the book.

An entry on the first page made the cabby tear up. "I had a feeling," the cabby said, looking at Jim.

"A feeling?" Jim asked.

"Yeah, a feeling I had worked on this very aircraft." The cabby pointed to a small script in the book.

"Do you see this?" the cabby asked. Jim stared into his log book.

"Yes. It's a clearance of a maintenance performed on that date."

"Those are my initials," he revealed. With a huge sigh the cabby left the cabin and stood outside admiring the skin on the plane.

"I'll be damned, the same plane, after all these years, she's still flying. I never thought I'd see the day one of my planes would ever come back this way. Now here one is."

"And this is your plane?" he asked Jim.

"Yes, it is," Jim told him as the two exchanged some of the history and idiosyncrasies of the plane. Jim made sure to tell the old fella,

"Those things have all been taken care of." He looked at the cabby and confessed,

"I find your story fascinating and I thank you for the interest in my plane, but we need to get airborne and headed back to Rhode Island while I can still cheat some of this sundown. Perhaps when I return, we can continue our conversation. Thanks again, goodbye."

They boarded the plane and watched the evening's red glow slowly fade to black. They descended onto the beacon at North Central and parked the plane at Jim's hangar. Harry and Ellie stayed the night with Jim and Liz and called for their tickets back to Shreveport in the morning.

Liz and Ellie stayed inside while Jim and Harry went out to the back deck. Liz was happy her son was beginning to settle into a life with someone he could love. She hoped a grandchild would come along shortly.

Jim was taken by Ellie's beauty. He told arryHarry Harry Harry, "You did very well for yourself, Harry. She is a lovely woman and you two make a fine looking couple. I wish you all the luck, Harry, and good luck on your career."

"Jim…I had that same gut feeling with Ellie. That feeling I had with Ollie…in the gut? Ellie had it too."

"Oh, so that's why it works." A light breeze was wafting across the yard.

"Have you been getting any calls yet for any R & D work, Harry? With your background and credentials, I should wonder why they haven't. Oh, well. It's their loss. Enjoy where you are, Harry. You've done well."

"Thanks, Jim. It's early yet, we've only been married a couple of weeks. Ellie's business is doing very well with people calling all the time. She's had to turn away some because her calendar is full, and several days a month are set aside for personal time, or so people can call in case of an emergency. Pretty soon she's going to need a switchboard."

"You know your mother is happy, now that your married, and there's going to be somebody there, by your side, when you need them." Jim told him.

"And Mom is happy with you, Jim. That means an awful lot to me, not just to mom. She's been lonely since my father died. Lonely inside. She has a lot of friends, but they don't take care of the deep and the truly personal side of a relationship."

The next morning, as they boarded the plane at T.F Green, Harry almost forgot to ask,

"Don't forget to call us when the wedding is. I don't want to miss it."

"I'll let you know, Harry. Bye, Ellie. Have a safe trip, you two."

Harry blew a kiss to his mother, and for a moment, Liz thought she felt it. She drew back thinking someone had come up behind her, or that Jim did it, but she was watching Jim, standing in front of her.

"I never felt something like that before," she thought.

"Something like what, honey?"

"Oh, it was nothing, I guess. For a moment, I thought I could feel the kiss Harry had blown to me."

"You are going to miss them, dear. You should feel something. Let's go home."

CHAPTER 23

Keep Going

Harry's career as a B-52 pilot ended when history got a little too close for comfort and repeated itself. During a return flight over Eastern Europe, as they were photographing the Western border of the Soviet Union, something broke causing the bomb bay doors on the plane to open, at 30,000 feet.

"Jackson, why do I have a light on up here telling me the bomb bay doors are open?"

"I don't know sir. I'll look into it." Master Sgt. Robert Jackson was flight engineer. After checking all the possible electrical connections that could malfunction, all the mechanicals that could come loose, he left his seat to check on the doors.

"Yep. I don't know why, Colonel, but she's wide open."

"Well, find out what the hell is going on and fix it. We're flying with our zippers down. We are exposed to the Russians."

"I'll get right on it, Sir."

Sgt. Jackson put his parachute on and went down into the bomb bay. Tech. Sgt. and radio operator, Al Penny, went back to see Jackson didn't fall. When he got to the door Sgt. Jackson was gone.

"He's gone, sir. Sgt. Jackson is gone!" Penny yelled into his microphone.

"What the hell do you mean Jackson's gone? I just talked to him. He couldn't have gone anywhere else on the ship but back to his seat." Harry heard this story before, about a bombardier that nearly fell 30,000 feet over Viet Nam. It was his father. Now he had to come to grips with the fact that he just lost a crew member. One of his crew had just fallen from his ship, 30,000 ft to who knows where below.

"If he survives the fall an opens his chute, I hope he lands in friendly territory and not in Russian hands."

"Can you close the doors, Al?" he asked Sgt. Penny.

"I'll try, sir." Penny went down into the bay and saw what he thought was a loose fastener. He tightened it with his fingers as best he could and climbed back into the plane.

"Try it now, sir." he called up front, and he watched the doors close.

"Jackson will fall more than 10,000 ft in less than a minute. He has got to open his chute." Harry called command to report what happened. They told him to abort the mission since he had been 'exposed'. He turned the plane around to go back to base, deflated that he had lost a man. Ordinarily it would be an improbable thing to have happen. But he remembers what General Reynolds told him about his father. If it hadn't been Sgt. Charles Gamer, Harry would have never been born.

Harry received orders to land in England. The Command wanted to examine the bomb bay doors to make sure they were repairable. Radio traffic was being monitored of a parachute seen over the skies of Luhansk, Ukraine, 20 km from the Russian border.

Peasant farmers spotted the collapsed chute billowing in a potato field. They saw no movement. A farmer rushed out and at once recognized the American flag on the airman's shoulder. He told his son,

"Go back and get the wagon, before Russian troops reach this area." The Russians were known to sneak into Ukraine from time to time to steal food and harass the women. The farmer knew if the American or any of his equipment was found, they would search every farm in the area until they brought an American spy back to

Moscow. The soldiers' weapons were no match for the farmers', and they rarely resisted. No one would know if the prisoner would even survive the trip to Moscow. The Russians would deny any knowledge of his existence.

Local government authorities were notified as well as the US Ambassador and the President of Ukraine in Kyiv. Helicopters and ground troops were dispatched to the area to rescue Sgt. Robert Jackson. He woke staring up at a young woman wearing a babushka, trying to feed him. "Eat," she pleaded.

The girl's father told Jackson, "You must be quiet. Russian soldiers come. Now eat. Your government has been notified. They are sending men to pick you up. You will hide here until they come. We will know what to do with the Russians."

Jackson waited 6 hours for a convoy from the Ukraine Army to arrive from Kharkiv. From there he would be flown to Kyiv and arrangements made to get him back to his crew in the UK.

Harry and his crew were notified that Jackson had been rescued in the Ukraine. The dispatched mentioned a request by the Soviet government to help in find several of their soldiers that had strayed across the border while on patrol. No reports of lost soldiers being found in that area had been taken.

When Harry got back to the states and home in Shreveport, he put in his papers for retirement from the Air Force. When the general found out he called Harry into the office.

"Are you sure about this, Colonel Ackworth? You're bordering on a career that will make you a General. If you hold out another year, I'm positive they'll be tacking stars on your collar."

"That incident with a man out the bomb bay, sir, hit too close to home. It's a repeat of my father's incident during Viet Nam. It's time for me to hang up my wings and think about another career."

"You won't hang up your wings, you love flying too much, Harry. But if you're sure, I'll sign your papers, and I'll try to push them through."

"I would appreciate that, General. Thank you, sir."

"Protocol is protocol, I know, but let's cut the bullshit, Harry. We've known each other long enough to be frank and honest. Oh,

I can find a pilot to take your place. Hell, I've got a stack of officers waiting to get into the cockpit but none of them as cocky or savvy as you behind the wheel. Personally, I'm going to miss you, Harry, but you know I wish you the best of luck out there. You've got the experience and the foresight to tackle any position in the aviation world. Shit, how could you fail?"

"Good Luck, Brigadier Gen. Harry Ackworth. Send me a post card from where-ever you land."

Harry suddenly stopped his exit. He turned to face the General and ask,

"Excuse me, sir. Did I hear you say Brigadier General?"

"I knew you'd hear that, Harry. I'm sorry I didn't tell you right off. I wanted the opportunity to try to keep you in the Air Force."

"Thank you, sir. I really appreciate your words of encouragement, bullshit or not, but after 35 years, the duty stations around the globe, and all the new changes occurring…"

"I know you've had a full career, one you can be very proud of, and a career the Air Force is very proud to have had you, but I thought all the new changes would be the ones you couldn't turn down. I need a leader to spearhead these changes, Harry, understand what they are and where they go…how to put them in place and in action, without hesitation."

"Thanks for the vote of confidence, George, but the kids coming up today are way ahead of old dogs like you and me. We met the challenges with muscle. These new kids are meeting them with brains and one and zeros. It's too much for me for the changes occurring in my life. You know how it is when retirement looks you in the eye. Things look very different, and retirement looks very good. That's where I am George."

"I envy the plan that fate is handing you, Harry. You see and understand the hand she's dealt you and you're going to play it. In all our friendship, Harry, I wish you luck and good fortune."

In complete military pride and protocol, they exchange salutes, shake an honest, friendship filled handshake, and Harry turns and makes his way home.

The drive home was filled with reflection; with the laughter of the good times with the friends he's made, with the tears of the friends he's lost in testing new aircraft, and pride in the tests he helped come to successful endings. He quietly walked in the door and found Ellie prepping dinner. Turning her around to face him, he asked, "Do you want to go home?"

"You mean, 'home' home, like in Attleboro, Massachusetts home?"

"That home." He said firmly.

"What did you do, Harry?" She asked.

"I put in my papers, Ellie. I'll be a civilian in less than a month, and I will no longer be a colonel."

"Just a civilian, huh?" she asked.

"No. Now it's Brigadier General Harry Ackworth."

"Wow, Brigadier General? Harry that's wonderful. Tell me what that means."

"More money in my retirement check, basically. There aren't any more benefits, insurance-wise, than a private gets, unless you pay for it," he tells her.

"But I thought we were going to talk about this, Harry?"

"I'm sorry, hon, but that incident with Sgt. Jackson, even though it worked out alright, and the changes coming down the line…tomorrow's Air Force will be manned by the kids sitting in front of televisions with video games. That's not me, and I can't stop men falling out of bomb bay doors. It's time. Don't you think it's time, after 35 years?"

"I guess you're right, dear. But you do recognize the Air Force couldn't blame you for any wrongdoing in the Jackson Jump incident."

"'Jackson Jump'? No, he didn't jump, honey. He fell. It was an accident."

"Oh, I understand, and as scary as it was for Sgt. Jackson, now the men have a name for when something like that happens… besides calling it a malfunction of the plane," as she explained it.

"That's what scares me, Ellie, the unpredictability. That kind of thing happened to my father, 50 years ago, and now, me? I can't wait to see it happen to my son."

"It won't happen to our son, Harry. He won't be flying B-52's in his future. Those old relics have to retire. You know that."

"So now what, Retired Brigadier General Harry Ackworth… what are you going to do now? You can't stay home and bug the crap out of me. You'll force me to go back to work. You love flying too much to stay home."

"Yes, I do. I have to get back in the cockpit, but in a different uniform," Harry added.

"Well, start searching for left seat positions elsewhere. Get a copy of the Aviation Journal and start looking at job listings. Search the internet and see what you can come up with."

"I'll start looking at places with airports in the neighbor-hood," Ellie added.

"I wonder what's in the Attleboro area. I know North Central isn't that far off. The houses are nice, the schools are good, and the hospitals are first rate." Harry said.

"Get a job first, Harry. We will go where the job is," Ellie pointed out.

"I can fly just about anything, And I can figure out any problem you run into in the air. I am very good at that, Ellie." He paused and thought a moment but wasn't able to come up with an alternative."

"You don't want aerospace? They have been reaching out to you, with lucrative offers, on your terms."

"I know, but it would take me out of the cockpit and stick me at a drawing board. My ideas are too wild for them, Elli. They'd wind up on the stockpile of wild ideas. I don't know, if after more than 35 years, I can give up the left seat that easily. I love it so much. You know that."

"You don't want to work in the Skunk Works? The experimen-tal, secret hide-away, airplane developing, underground garage the Air Force has?"

"I can see you've seen some of this stuff on TV. But our titles are a little too long, honey."

"I just thought you might enjoy the challenge, so I watched a couple of episodes."

"I'm going to leave it to the kids coming up in the field. With all the AI being used, and new AI everyday they will be the only ones capable of keeping up with the changes. We, old dogs, our best challenge is with stick and rudder.

"Okay. How about a corporate pilot? You can fly the latest and the greatest business jets in the world. In fact, you can see the world from a different perspective. You'll be able to get out of the plane and see the cities you've been flying over at ground level. And maybe I can go with you."

"Ah-h-h!" he said. "Me thinks there be an ulterior motive working here."

"I see both sides of this coin, Elli. A great job, with great pay and a chance for you and me to see the world. And what do we do with the kids?"

"Harry!" she exclaimed. "Don't you remember attending William's graduation from the Academy."

"Yes. I'll never forget that day. The way our son introduced me to his friends. How he led off with, 'Do you know the story of the B-52 that lost a crew member out the bomb bay?' Then he would point to me and proudly announce, "Meet the pilot of that B-52, my father, Colonel Harry Ackworth." Oh, I remember."

"And our daughter, Virginia, the child I've always said was her father's daughter, do you remember her? The Navy has accepted her at Annapolis. She leaves in two weeks, and as she is the spitting image of her father, inside and out, I don't expect we will see much of her for four years, unless we go to Annapolis."

"I didn't forget that either. I guess I'll start looking for a pilot's seat somewhere."

"Do you still want to go home?" She asked.

"Yeah. Mom and Jim aren't getting any younger. And your mother, I'm sure, would like to see us more often now that your father is gone. Maybe we can take her on one of our trips. I don't think she would mind seeing Ireland again, do you?" Harry suggested.

"No, I don't think she would. And I seem to remember how you and mom liked that one pub. What was the name of that place?" Ellie asked.

"I don't remember, dear, but I'm sure your mother and I could find it," Harry mentioned.

"I'm sure. You best get busy searching for the job. I'll get on the internet and find us a home."

Harry retired from the Air Force as a Brigadier General, leaving behind the reputation as an Ace, but also the pilot that lost a man in flight. His reputation was saved by Gen. Reynolds at Embry-Riddle when he tells the story of the father and son team and the bomb bay doors on a B-29 and a B-52.

Harry did find a left seat job opening flying a Bombardier Global 7500 for a company based out of a small town in New Hampshire. He was amazed the airport had a runway as long as it was. 'It won't take a-52," he thought, "but it'll handle a 7500."

The company was international, supplying ball bearings for industry and the military. Harry loved the plane, and with Ellie, they were able to tour the world wherever he was scheduled to fly.

Two years after graduation, Harry's son was assigned to an air wing at a new and secret base in Maine. Harry knew the B-52 was being phased-out, retired to the Arizona desert because of age and a myriad of mechanical issues too expensive to correct or repair. The modern age of super stealth warfare led his son to pilot the B-21 Raider Bomber.

"Did you get a front seat?" Harry asked.

"You wouldn't believe it dad. I qualified for more than they needed or wanted. You know, they didn't have to ask me twice."

"How is it?"

"She's a computer with a bomb rack, dad. It flies so well you hardly know you're in the air. We rarely fly during the day, mostly at night. That way we are not seen coming and going on our missions. The base is not very big, but access is 5 miles from any main road. Security!"

"Don't tell me anymore, son. You don't want to risk a security breach, and neither of us wants to lie, unless we're caught by the enemy."

"So, what are you doing now, dad? Is retirement getting to you yet?"

"Oh, I'm no longer retired, son. Your mother didn't think I could stay out of a left seat for very long. She was right. I applied for a seat as a corporate pilot. I jockey around the big wigs of a multinational ball bearing manufacturer."

"And what are you flying? A Citation, a Lear?"

"Nope. The company has a Bombardier Global 7500. Son, it is a dream; fly's high, fly's fast, and serves coffee. It just doesn't have the stealth capabilities your ride has. I love it."

"That's good to hear, dad. I know how complete you are with things, especially your flying," Bill added.

"Your grandfather taught me that, son. It would have been great if you could have met him. He taught me so many things; the right things to do in life. I tried to pass them on to you. I hope you pass them on to your kids when it comes time."

"Mom told me you have this thing with wings. What was she talking about?"

"When I was growing up, my father would take me out hunting or fishing, or anything we could do together, I always took that time to talk to him personally. I would tell him what was bothering me. He would sit me down and look me in the eye, then tell me,

"Son, you have to play the hand life deals you, and you have to play it honestly, being fair and square with everybody, cause you're not getting off this earth until your wings are done. Unless you do something stupid. Then you don't know what kind of wings you're going to get."

William looked at his father and asked,

"Were grandpa's wings done?"

"I think so but let me add…they were done much too soon. There was an auto accident when he was called and he went quickly, with not much pain. Your grandmother was glad of that. He called to her in the end, saying,

"I guess my wings are ready." Kissed her, closed his eyes, and that was it. The doctor said the injuries from the accident caused his death. My mother didn't believe that, because my father was awake and talking to her when he closed his eyes." Harry told him.

"So, you do the best you possibly can. Treat everybody you meet fairly and squarely, being completely honest with them. Give 100%, why give less. The people deserve it, and you feel better afterward. You worked hard trying to get the most out of your schooling and putting that education to good use. You gave Uncle Sam 100%? And your employer 100%? Everybody deserves 100%".

"I can see you are right, dad," William said, "but I can see I still have more to give."

"Got a steady girl, son?"

"No, dad, I don't. I'm in no hurry. I go out on dates, sure, but occasionally. If she's out there, she'll show up. I'll wait."

"Let me tell you one thing, son, which might help. The one that steals your heart may come by accident, not by intent. She may not stay long because her wings may be ready. And you will hurt, tremendously, and it won't go away until someone comes along to erase that pain. Accept the pain, that uneasy feeling. One young lady may come along and tell you she's got that same uneasy feeling. Pay attention, that person could be your mate for the rest of your life.

If she says anything about wings, hold onto her. She will be the right one, maybe not for long…"

"Only until her wings are ready," Bill said, wondering.

"Exactly. I think that's why my father pointed it out so well… being honest with everybody. Treating them fairly and squarely, because you never know when your wings will be done. And you know, less is not fair, to anyone. Not fair to you either. Don't worry about your wings. Someone else is taking care of that.

"Nuts, I have to go, son. I'm taking your mother out to supper. No fighting with your sister."

"Dad, she's in college. She knows what she's doing."

"Oh, yeah. Well, don't wait up. We could be late."

William knew late for his mother and father was only after a late movie, maybe 10:00PM, but this was only a dinner.

"They'll be home by 9:00PM."

C H A P T E R 2 4

The Last Word With Angels

George asked Alexander if Harry's wings were ready.

"Oh, no, not Harry's wings, not Ellie's. We've got more feathers to add to his wings before they're done. And Ellie will go along with him. You know the rules, I can't say anymore, even among us.

"George…you're asking questions you shouldn't ask. Even if I knew, I wouldn't be able to tell you. Besides, love and marriage, pickles and ice cream, mother screams, baby screams, father pulls his hair out. It will go on and on forever and ever. And it's up to the Boss anyway. I'm glad we don't have to build any baby wings. I hate that."

"So, are we on break now?"

"Unfortunately, no, George. I got an order from upstairs. The Boss wants us to start on two sets of wings, one for a pilot, one for his wife. I'll let you take it from there."

"I think I know who they are for. How soon does he want them?" George wondered.

147

"Christmas time." Alexander said.

"Oh, what a bad time of the year. I mean, it's a great time, up here, to give someone their wings. But it's a bad time down there for people. Can I ask you who the pilot is?"

Alexander shows George the work order and the two names on it.

"No? Really? Well, life has been good to them. I'll see they're done on time."

CHAPTER 25

Wings of History

Harry and Ellie were enjoying their evening out. They were some distance from home and were hungry when they arrived in Newport, Rhode Island. They walked out on the movie, telling the ticket agent, "That wasn't worth the money." But dinner was special, it was Ellie's birthday, and Harry planned a whole night just for her. He made reservations at the club hosting big bands at the Newport Yacht Club. It was a 10:00 PM show and there was still time to walk the pier and ga-ga at the expensive boats.

The night was filled with stars and the temperature quite comfortable. There were so many boats, so many expensive boats, all so alluring. The couple made note of this boat with the tall mast, and that boat with the three decks. They saw deck hands in uniforms on some of the boats and people in street clothes, shorts and sandals, on others.

"These are some of the 'beautiful people,' Harry told her. Their reservation placed their table within 8ft of the band. Harry and Ellie picked up the vibe to get up on the dance floor a few times, and after their lobster dinner, the bandmaster asked the people to stand and wish Ellie a happy birthday with singing. The cook brought out a small three layer cake and Ellie wrapped her arms around Harry's neck and gave him a big kiss. There was a loud crescendo and the crash of cymbals and drums.

The band master, Howard Makin, came down and offered Ellie happy birthday with a kiss on the cheek. Harry got up and shook Makin's hand, palming him $200 for seeing the smile on Ellie's face. Makin was a classmate of Harry's from the Air Force Academy, but music was Howard's dream, not planes. Harry and Ellie listened and danced to the big bands until 1:00 AM when they checked into their room at the Harbor Hotel. Harry called home knowing William would worry but was surprised that William, himself, hadn't called. His phone rang, Bill answered,

"Hello, Bill. Surprised the old folks aren't home yet like we should be?"

"Well, yeah, dad. I was wondering where you two had gone. It is late, you know, but I can stay up, I'm 18 and I'm out of high school."

"That's all true, son, but there is one important thing you did forget today." Harry told him.

"What was that dad?"

"Look at the calendar. What does it say?"

Bill's eyes popped out when he realized he had forgotten his mother's birthday. "Geeze Dad, why didn't you remind me?"

"I had enough on my mind keeping this evening secret from your mother, and she is having a wonderful time, as am I, watching her. We will be staying overnight in Newport and be home sometime tomorrow, probably in the afternoon. You don't have to worry. Good night, son."

"Yeah, goodnight, dad. Have fun, see you tomorrow, some-time."

Breakfast was a simple affair and Ellie was over the top from last night's celebrating. Harry felt he owed it to her after all the years he was away at 30,000ft. After breakfast they headed back to Attleboro going through different neighborhoods, some they had never seen before. Ellie was thinking a smaller house would be nice to retire in. She and Harry had discussed retiring to the southern coast or the Left Coast, but they knew the food would never be the same. They felt they were hardy New Englanders and enjoyed the ambiance of the Maine, New Hampshire, and Massachusetts coastline.

Turning down one street after another, they never realized just how far south they had gone until the Greenwich Bay north shore. The big house in Attleboro wasn't needed anymore. "I want something smaller, Harry, more intimate, just for you and me. I'll take two bedrooms, maybe an unfinished cellar."

Harry gave her a, "Ditto. Maybe room for a boat…a small boat?"

"We can do that. Let's keep looking," Ellie said.

They rode through the different neighborhoods where it showed the people cared about their property, with mowed lawns, no junk cars visible from the street. Ellie spotted a small Cape that looked like it met all their requirements and appeared to be well cared for. A for sale sign was in the window, but before inquiring about it, they rode around the immediate area, looking for the schools, the churches, the grocery stores. How long would it take for the fire department or the police to arrive? They liked the area and noted a gas station only a block away.

"This looks good Harry," Ellie told her husband.

As they drove back around the neighborhood, a real estate agent was posting a sign from her agency saying the house was for sale. Harry and Ellie stopped in front of the house and asked the agent about it.

"Hello," Ellie cried out. "When did the house go on the market?"

"Why, just today. Are you interested?" the agent asked.

"Frankly, yes," Ellie told her. She turned around to wave at Harry, whispering, "Come see the house, Harry."

"Your husband seems somewhat reluctant."

"Shopping of any kind is not his thing. He always stays in the car when I walk into a store. I'll get him in here," Ellie said.

"Harry, come see the house." Harry got out of the car and locked it. The agent told him, "You don't have to worry about your car here, sir. This is a very good neighborhood. There are no children living in this park. Oh, you must have missed the sign out front as you entered the park. This is a retirement community, only 60 and over can apply for housing here. You are both 60, and over? The agent asked.

"Yes, I'm afraid so," Ellie told her.

"Don't be ashamed of your age. It's because you meet the requirements that we are even talking. Let's go inside and I'll show you around."

The agent was a middle aged woman, attractive, slender, with white hair. Harry thought, somewhat 'stately' looking. She must know her stuff. The agent took them up to the bedrooms, 2 large rooms with separate baths. The cellar had been prepped and partitioned for two more rooms, similar to the main floor. 'Nice,' Harry thought. 'Someone has begun the work for me.'

The first floor was expansive. The joint living/dining room with an open concept leading to the kitchen gave the appearance of a much larger home, uncluttered. Harry and Ellie fell in love with it. The price was good. They could meet it, but they had to sell the two story colonial first. The agent told Harry and Ellie she could be their home as well. It had to be the fastest sale the agent ever made. The owners of the home were an elderly couple getting ready for a retirement/assisted living community. They welcomed Harry and Ellie and thanked them for buying their home so quickly.

The contract told both parties are to vacate their premises within 45 days. Harry thought, plenty of time to know what's coming with them, and what's staying in the old house or being tossed. Harry and Ellie had a much easier time deciding than the elderly couple. There were too many memories remaining in the home they hated to part with them, only because there was no room for their things at the community they were moving to. Harry approached them saying,

"Why don't we do this? Because you can only bring so much with you for lack of space, why don't you leave some things here. Ellie and I can store them in the cellar and when you're ready for them, we will be happy to help you retrieve them. How does that sound?"

"That is very nice of you, son," the elderly gentleman said. He was a few years older than his wife, not too proud to brag that he had just celebrated his 92nd birthday.

"Congratulations," Harry told him, then asked, "Do you happen to have any cake left?"

"Harry!" Ellie exclaimed. "You don't ask for cake."

"I was joking."

"That's quite alright. I was as brash and forward once, and I'll bet you were in the Air Force. Am I right?"

"Well, yes. Yes, I was. I retired a year ago. How could you tell?"

"When I saw the contract for the sale, and the name Harry Ackworth, I started putting things together; name, age, haircut," the old man pointed to Harry's buzz cut. "To me it added up to Air Force."

"Oh," Harry asked, "I don't look like Special Forces or Green Beret, not buff enough?"

The old fella cocked his head and jokingly said, "No, son. The man I once served with in the Pacific had a last name of Ackworth, Oliver Ackworth. You have some of his facial features, I think."

The old man's wife chimed in, "Sam, it's been too long."

"Yes, my dear it has. Tell me, do you remember your grandfather?" the man asked.

"No, I don't. My father never spoke of him. I think he died immediately after my father was born."

The old man laughed inside, saying to himself, "No, he died before you were born."

"Your grandfather was in the Air Force, and I'll bet your father was in the Air Force, too, wasn't he?" the old gent asked.

"George, don't pester these folks with your war stories."

"He's quite right, mam."

"Oh, you can call me Olivia, none of that mam stuff. I had enough of that when Sam was in the Air Force," she said.

Harry and Ellie jumped a little inside to hear the name Olivia.

"But I must tell you, I did not know my grandfather. No one ever spoke of him while I was growing up. I never saw a picture of him or my grandmother. They had both passed before I was born. May I ask how you knew my father and grandfather, sir?"

"Call me Sam. Your grandfather and I served in the Air Force during the early days of the Korean War. He was a pilot on an F-86. I did the maintenance on his plane. We graduated from the schools the Air Force sent us to, but afterwards, your grandfather made the decision to fly, so he became a pilot. I stayed to further my education on the F-86. We had some grand times in Colorado, he and I."

"That was where he met your grandmother, Alice Johnson, a very pretty woman, wasn't she dear?"

Olivia nodded with some resignation, as she carried in a tray of cake and coffee. She had heard the story a hundred times before, Sam always mentioning how pretty Alice was.

"It was an odd coming together, those two. We had dated one night, the four of us, going to the club. We were going to listen to the big bands. The restaurant was serving a special Colorado beef steak for next to nothing, one night only, they said. So, we show up and go to our table, right up front, beautiful. You could reach out and touch the band. After the meal, which was great as I remember, right Olivia?"

"Oh, it was a delicious meal. The first time I had steak, and it was wonderful. We went back…"

"Okay, that's enough, dear." Harry looked at Ellie as she laughed at the old gent's reaction to his wife.

"All of a sudden Alice gets a stomach-ache. "I have to leave," she says. Halfway to her place, your grandfather, Oliver, gets the same stomach-ache. Olivia and me, we were fine, no stomach-ache. The next morning comes and we're going out to breakfast. They meet at her place, and she says she felt a pain all night long. Oliver says he did, too. But strangely, they didn't have that pain when they were together. Ollie and I looked at one another and said, Love Pain."

Ollie explained it to them, and they agreed. They didn't ask any questions. They looked at one another and said together, 'let's get married.'

"In that week, we had a great meal while listening to a fantastic band. They get sick, get married, and we see them off on a honeymoon to the Islands. When they got back Oliver and I receive orders to report. The Korean War had started, and we jumped into training. Me, the mechanic. Your grandfather, the F-86 pilot. We didn't see much of one another while training, but in Korea, we were both assigned to the same wing. I was placed in charge of the maintenance on his plane. It was great for about six months."

Sam paused in his story telling, tipped his head up a little and took a faraway look, saying, "I remember that day like it was yesterday." Harry watched as a tear fell down Sam's cheek.

Olivia brought out a tray of birthday cake and coffee, with the excuse, "We didn't get many to come to Sam's party. Most of our friends are gone now, so there's plenty of cake. Have as much as you like." She looked at her husband and knew he was having a flashback; an action packed, live screen look, back to 1951. "Sam. Come back, Sam."

"I haven't gone anywhere, my dear old friend." Sam looked at Harry and Ellie, sacrificing the words in a whisper,

"The pain never goes away. It's not as sharp, but it never goes away."

"You don't have to say anymore, Sam," Harry told him.

"No, after all these years, to meet the grandson of one of the bravest men I have ever known. It is an honor. You should know these things of your grandfather." He took hold of Harry's hand and moved closer, more intimately, and began again.

"We arrived at Suwon Air Base in late July of 1951. The rainy season had just ended, and though the days were beginning to warm up, the red clay of the region still remained tacky, making it difficult to get around. Anyway, the F-86 your grandfather flew was a remarkable plane. Oliver told me he met Chuck Yeager in flight school, learned a few things."

"By December of that year, United Nations forces had discovered a hidden base where the North Korean's were staging most of their fighters. Until the F-86 arrived we were losing too many planes and men. It really helped to even the score, so to speak."

"Your grandfather was a phenomenal pilot, with great instinct and reflex. He also had a great deal of luck riding with him every time he went up. And every time he came back, I would have more holes to patch in his plane. He had me paint his kills over some of the bullet patches. I told him it would make his plane look like a target."

"He kept telling me he wasn't going anywhere until his wings were done. I would ask him what that meant, all he would do is wink at me. I found out later, after he was shot down, what it meant. I can still see him strapping in for that last time. He looked at me with that wad of gum between his teeth and told me, "It might be today, Ollie. It might be today.""

"I watched him lift off, but he never came back. A recon patrol found his plane. The cockpit, they said, was riddled with bullet holes, but they never found a body." His wingman reported Oliver shot down two Migs before the third took him down." Sam sipped his coffee but didn't touch his cake.

"Ah, I've had enough cake. You can have it, son," he told Harry. "And we are very proud to be selling you this house."

"After that story, I don't know if I can live up to the reputation you've laid in its foundation."

"Those are kind words, Harry, but now, after meeting you and your wife, I have something else for you. Wait here."

Harry looked at Olivia, wondering what her husband was up to. Sam came back carrying a photo album with '1950-1952 Korea' stamped on the cover.

"I want to give this to you, Harry. It's everything I have about my time with your grandfather and grandmother Alice. Our children don't want any of this stuff," Sam said, waving around the room. "And our grandchildren are stuck in today's world of A.I., video games, and drugs. They are not interested in their personal history, as much as we have tried to bring it back to them."

"Thank you, Sam. I'm sorry about your children and grandchildren not wanting to get in touch with their roots. I will cherish this album, Sam, Olivia. Ellie and I would like to see you again to go over these photos with you, not to bring back old, painful memories, but to help me, us, understand our past. I have a son who is a bomber pilot in the Air Force and a daughter about to graduate from the Annapolis."

"You've done a great job with your children and a wonderful thing for your country. Congratulations to you, both. Shamefully we cannot say as much for our children or grandchildren, but there is still time for redemption."

Sam got up, holding Harry's arm as he led us to the door. "I will send you our new address so we can get together to discuss these bits of history. That would be fun. And we will be out in 45 days as in the contract. We have to be at our new place by then. Thank you, again, for stopping to see the house and for the sale."

As the door closed behind them, Harry and Ellie stood back to look at the house. "It's going to be a fine home for us, Ellie."

"Yes, Harry, it will…until our wings are done."

CHAPTER 26

New Beginnings

That fall before the 45 days had past, Ellie and Harry, Sam and Olivia had moved into their new homes. Harry and Ellie to Greenwich Bay and Sam and Olivia to West Ocean Assisted Living in west Cranston. Some of Sam's things were kept in the cellar of the home on Greenwich Bay. Boxes of little things they no longer wanted were placed on the curb and marked free. Harry and Ellie did the same in selling their two story home. It seemed like the thing to do for so many folks moving out of different neighborhoods. Sam and Olivia did sell a few items they couldn't take with them for lack of space. The money was placed in their account for their living expenses at West Ocean.

Harry and Ellie walked around many boxes throughout the home before finding a place for everything. Harry wondered,

"I hope Sam and Olivia are comfortable at West Ocean. It's a terrible thing having to move at their age, after being here for so many years."

"We will have to visit them, Harry, after a time, let them settle in, and maybe we can invite them for supper one night," Ellie suggested.

"I would like that. Sam has important history of my family I need to copy down. I have the album, but pictures only say so much. I need his memories."

"And I think Olivia and I would have a few things to talk about. It would be fun."

Jim and Liz paid a surprise visit to the new tenants on Greenwich Bay. Harry and Ellie didn't know they were coming and were more surprised when Jim pulled into the yard towing their boat.

"Mom, Jim, hey, great to see you." Jim parked the boat, and then he and Liz went in to see the new house.

"This is nice, Ellie, Harry. Just the right size. It certainly is cozier than the colonial you had."

"Yes, we like the way the previous owner opened up this area. It makes the house much more spacious. And we don't need all that floor space to negotiate going room to room. I have to tell you, mom, the old couple we bought the house from, the man is 92. He served with my grandfather in Korea. He even gave me a photo album of pictures of my grandfather and grandmother. It's only dated 1950 to 1952 but it has lots of photos and newspaper prints of the day."

"I would like to see that, Harry. That would fill in a great deal of our family history."

The four shared the album and a meal before Jim and Liz revealed the real reason they came to visit. Jim handed Harry a wrapped box about the size of a bar of soap.

"What's this? A gift? What for, it's not my birthday or any special occasion," Harry said in surprise.

"Open it, Harry," Jim asked.

"Okay." Harry took the wrapping off and opened the box. Inside he found the keys to the boat Jim had just towed down and parked in Harry's driveway.

"Are these the keys to your boat, Jim?"

"No, they are the keys to your boat, now."

"Why are you giving us your boat?" Harry asked.

Jim paused before giving the explanation. Shyly, not sure how Harry was going to take the answer, he asked Harry to, "Take a walk with me son. Ellie, would you go with Liz?"

"Wait a minute, Jim. Is it bad news? Ellie and I can take it together. Please, tell us what it is."

"Your mother and I are not in good health. In the past year, we've been seeing oncologists."

"Cancer specialists? Both of you? How do two people in one house come down with cancer at the same time? That is the most unfortunate thing I have ever heard. Mom? What kind of cancer do you have?"

"Ovarian, dear. It's malignant and has metastasized into my liver and kidneys." Liz hung her head and began to weep. Ellie wrapped her arms around her.

Harry turned to Jim with a frightened look. "And what is it you want to tell us, Jim?"

"I have also been diagnosed with a cancer common in men... Prostate cancer, but mine is of a particular aggressive nature. The doctors can't seem to get hold of it. It's now in my colon and spreading." Jim got up and walked outside to the dock. Harry followed but with some hesitancy. He stopped to look at his mother in Ellie's arms.

"Jim? Mom?" Harry said loudly, "What does all this mean?"

Liz told her son, "It means Jim and I are dying, and as I have done your whole life, Harry, I could not pull any punches. I had to, Jim and I had to tell you the unvarnished truth. I'm sorry son."

Harry went out to see Jim. He stood at the end of the dock smoking a cigarette. Harry told him,

"Well, that's not going to help." Jim turned around,

"It's not going to make a difference, either. The doctor said we both have about 5 months, more if we undergo surgery and chemo and whole lot of other things to drag out the end. She and I have decided to ride it out to the end. No surgery, chemo, or other meds."

Harry admonished Jim for his cavalier approach.

"You can't do this, Jim. You and my mother have got to seek treatment."

"We have, Harry. For the past year we've been in and out of doctor's offices and hospitals and taken this pill and that drug, the both of us…only to come out with the same results. We've even asked the doctors to make sure the results were ours and not someone else's."

Harry collapsed to his knees, deflated. He looked at his mother and began to cry, helpless to stop the ravaging that was going on inside her and Jim.

"And now you want to get rid of things? What, legally give them away before someone else takes them? Why? And what's next, the *Gin?* What are you going to do with her?" he asked assertively.

"I was hoping you'd take her, Harry. You love being in the left seat and you know how to fly her. I know you'd take care of her. You realize her place in history." Jim pulled another set of keys from his pocket. They were for the Lockheed.

Harry saw the keys and stared at them, then looked into Jim's eyes, resigned to the coming future of his mother and Jim no longer being with them.

"This is a lot to take in on a sudden visit, don't you think, Jim?"

"Yeah, I know. Your mother and I talked about how we were going to tell you. On our way here, we thought about turning around to try to find another way. But your mother had a visit last night from your father. He told her…

> *"…to play the cards you are dealt, Liz, fairly and honestly. Don't give Harry anything but the truth. He knows how to take it. I'll be waiting for you and Jim."*

"Those are the words your mother said to me. I know the story of the wings and how they are supposed to be waiting for you. Frankly, Harry, if there are wings for me some-where, I'll take whatever the angels give me."

The sad mood began to shift and wane as the mention of wings began to take over. Harry and Jim went inside to see Liz and Ellie sitting at the counter with tea. He went to his mother and hugged her lovingly, not wanting to let go. Liz held him and said,

"It's alright, son. Jim and I are old now. It's time, in one way or another, for us to pick up our wings."

"Mom. You are not 80 yet. There is still plenty of time for us to enjoy life together. And you, Jim. What? You're 82? In that case I'm not far behind."

"But your wings are not ready yet, Harry, and neither are Ellie's. You live rightly, continue to do so, and you will see your grandchildren. Jim and I have come full circle. When the time comes it will be because our wings are completed."

"This is not going to go over well with William and Virginia. We have to find the right time to tell them. Bill is in Maine with his family, but he's probably at 35,000ft right now. And Virginia just graduated from Annapolis. She'll be home in a week, wanting to spend some time here and go up to visit you. We'll tell them before they visit."

Ellie asked, "Would you like to stay for dinner? Or perhaps go out tonight for seafood?"

Jim raised his hand at the seafood idea. "I do know this great little place, down the coast, where you can boat in and have a great time. They've got casual music, a great bar and the best seafood selection, cooked to perfection." He looked at Harry and said, "Let's get the boat in the water, Harry."

The four dressed for the 1 mile crossing to Goddard State Park. Jim drove into the channel aside Goddard and found a birth in front of *Fin's Dockside Mongiatorium*. Music could be heard as they traveled down the channel. The waitress gave them the option of staying in the boat or going ashore and sitting at a table. The table sounded best, and as it turned out, where they were able to rest their minds and accept what future they could see and play out their hands.

From the restaurant they walked the docks and along the shore, picking up stones, trying to make them skip across the glassy, still bay. Harry could hear the ladies talking softly in halting phrases. He and Jim simply walked the beach, dangling a cigarette. Every once in a while, one would find a seashell to comment on.

As the dark began to envelope the evening, they turned around to go back to the boat. When they reached Harry's landing, Jim parked the boat on the sand and through the anchor on the shore. They walked up the embankment and stood in the driveway wondering how to say goodnight. Harry wondered if he should say goodbye, but he let that pass and gave his mother a big hug and kissed her cheek. He walked up to Jim and hugged him and shook his hand asking,

"Please let us know when you are about to leave us. It would be the better way to play out our hands."

"I will do that, Harry. Your mother would want it that way, and I think I would, too. But you know, us military men don't care much for the formality of dying."

Harry nodded, wished them luck, and a fond goodbye.

CHAPTER 27

Tomorrows Wings

In early December, 5months after Jim and Liz paid their visit to Harry and Ellie, Liz passed from the cancer. Jim was in the hospital bed next to her, unconscious, his body ready to release him at any moment. When Jim passed, Harry sat alone in the room with his friend. He talked to Jim, saying thank you for his friendship, the love and devotion he paid to Liz, and the introduction to flying. He made note to being introduced to the Air Force, and especially the importance of keeping the classic planes, such as the Lockheed Electra, in the hearts and minds of the people today.

As he sat there speaking to Jim, he felt something brush by his face. He shooed it away, thinking it was a fly. The second time it happened, something stopped in front of him. Harry's eyes clouded until they were able to focus on a vision of his mother.

"Aw, ma," he voiced, tired from all the emotion he and Ellie had expired so recently.

"Alright, ma. I'm listening."

"I'm not here to alert you, warn you, give you advice, nothing, son. I've come back to get my husband. His wings are ready."

"Yours look nice, ma. Have you seen Ollie?"

"Yes, Harry, and she is doing fine. You'll laugh, I know, but she's playing cards with your father. But don't worry about her, Harry. Just take care of Ellie, and your children. Ake sure you show them the album, it's important for them to know their history."

While he was talking to his mother, Jim showed up wearing his wings. "Hello, Harry. Your mother and I were glad you and Ellie were by our side in the end. Both of us leaving within minutes of one another, that's tough. But you kept it together. Don't lose it after today. You've still got plenty of time to enjoy your children and grandchildren before you pick up your wings. Oh, I've seen your father, Harry. He's a nice guy. We get along well, but I won't play cards with him."

"Aren't you supposed to get along…up there?" pointing to the ceiling. "…and I know nothing of his card playing."

"Good. He's very sharp…and we do get along, yes."

Harry told his mother,

"I found your letter, mom. Ellie and I will honor your requests."

"Thank you, son. We have to go now. No need to worry about us, Harry, not up here. Call us when you need us. We'll drop by."

The visions faded as Ellie walked in.

"Hi, hon. I just saw mom and Jim."

"You spoke to your mother, and Jim?" ary told her

"Yeah," he said with some sobriety. "They're okay. They've got their wings."

"Yeah, I figured they'd be okay. Why not?"

"Mom's letter asked that she and Jim be cremated, together, and their ashes scattered from *Ginny's Gin.*"

"We can do that, Harry," Ellie told him, holding her husband in her arms. "When do you want to hold the service?"

"I think the funeral home will do the cremating tomorrow. We can hold a memorial service on Saturday, giving people the opportunity to get here. The ashes? We can scatter early Sunday morning, as they both asked."

Harry left the room, sullenly, and walked outside. He asked Ellie,

"Would you call the funeral home for me, dear?"

"Ok." Ellie called the home nearest Liz's home in Lincoln. Arrangements were made for a brief service to take place at the funeral home, a blessing service with a sprinkling of holy water. Jim and Liz did not want a church service. That's why they requested the ashes be scattered on Sunday morning.

Ellie made several phone calls while Harry was outside composing his emotions. She went outside to join him an found him staring up at the clouds.

"I wonder which one is theirs?" he asked Ellie.

She held his arm, feeling how much, he was going to miss his mother, and Jim. "It could be anyone of them, honey. But what do they do when there aren't any clouds?"

Harry looked down into Ellie's face and kissed her nose, laughing at her question.

"Let's go home," he said.

The answering machine at home was filled with condolences. Most of the calls could be dismissed but the one Harry didn't want to hear was from Billy.

"Mom, dad…I'm sorry I won't be there for the service. Duty calls and I have a plane to get in the air. I will ty to be down soon. I'm going to miss grandma and Jim. I'm sorry. Bye."

"He sounded like he wanted to be here," Harry said. "But I know how duty can get in the way of things we call important. We'll see him soon, I'm sure."

The next Saturday, at high noon, Jim's favorite western movie, droves of friends filled the funeral home. The words expressed by his former military buddies were filled with the patriotism Jim lived by his whole life. An honor guard surrounded the urn, and Harry was surprised to see Maj. General Harold Reynolds and General George Hancock. They brought the honor guard to represent the Air Force and the gratitude of the nation for Jim's service to his country. Generals Reynolds and Hancock gave a wonderful testimonial to Jim.

Harry teared up listening to the stories of the man he knew. "It was all so true," he told himself. Harry told his two senior executive officers what the plan was for Sunday morning. The generals said they would be there.

"I'm going up tomorrow, just after sunrise, in the Electra, to scatter their ashes."

"That's really nice, Harry. I think we'll stick around for the honor." Gen. Reynolds told him.

"Jim would like that, General."

The sun came up over Greenwich Bay at 5:04 and Harry felt the heat on his face. He woke Ellie and got the day started by driving to North Central Airport where *Ginny's Gin* was parked. Harry would fly the Electra to T.F. Green State Airport after a brief period of mourning. Jim had started the paperwork a month before he passed. The reading of the will would close the transaction.

As he pulled onto the apron in front of the garage, the generals were there with the honor guard. *Ginny's Gin* had been rolled out and the urn placed on the plane under guarded.

Harry went to the cockpit and hesitatingly took the left seat. Ellie and the honor guard strapped in by the door preparing the urn. The generals and the flag bearers stood at attention as Harry rolled down the runway. He circled the runway three times as he climbed to 5,000ft. The General Reynolds with binoculars watched the door open. He radioed a formation overhead to prepare to make their pass.

As Harry leveled off at 5,000 ft, he saw on his radar a blip getting closer and closer. He ordered the ashes be scattered just as the blip passed overhead. Harry gave a big grin and a let a proud tear fall, watching Billie, in the B-2 bomber, fly over, accompanied by an F-35 and an F-16. After the ashes were scattered the four planes landed at North Central, the Electra landing first, followed by the F-16, the F-35, and finally the B-2. They all rolled to a stop at the end of the tarmac in front of the Electra's hangar.

More personnel from around the state were called in to provide security for the flight. Crowds rushed down the apron to get a look at the mini airshow, especially the B-2, but were held back a minimum of 100 ft. Harry climbed out of the Electra and walked over to the B-2 to greet the pilot. He was not surprised to see his son climb out of the cockpit.

"Billy!" Harry called out and saluted. "Got your message, son. I am happy you could make it, more than happy this way. It was a great tribute."

Billy pointed to the generals walking toward them. Protocol called for a salute by all the junior officers as the general approached.

"You gentlemen have gone well beyond the limit in honoring our friend." As Harry was speaking, he saw another friend coming toward him, George Gamer, alone. Harry offered his hand, but George demanded a hug.

"I'm sorry about Vicky. We just couldn't get away. But your being here is a sure honor to Jim, above all the honor guards and the fly over.

"Thank you, Harry. Those are nice words. I could not stay away. Jim was a dear friend. Even with all I'm dealing with right now I had to come to say goodbye to my friend."

"I tried to call but could never get through." Harry told him.

"I've been having a tough time with Vicky gone. I don't always answer the phone. The General found me sucking down a cool one by the pool. He told me your plans and offered me a ride up. Of course, I said yes. There was no way I was going to miss a send-off to Jim. It was beautiful." George pointed to Billy,

"Nice plane you got there, but it's not like a -52."

"No," Billy answered with confidence. "It's not. It's better."

George smiled and all the men laughed. They all went into the hangar where they found a cooler filled with Jim's favorite beer, and a few other select brews. A caterer brought several trays of appetizers and sandwiches.

Harry was asked by General Reynolds what his plan were for the Electra.

"Well, I am going to fly it for a while when I'm not up in the Bombardier. Ellie and I will take it cross country, since that was one of the dreams my mother and Jim wanted to fulfill."

"She could bring you a wonderful price on the market, Harry."

"I know, but that money be Jim's money, not mine. No, Ellie and I want to see the Left Coast of sunny California, before it falls into the sea. We're both retired and have time to kill flying up and down the coast. I think she'll climb over the Rockies without a problem. That would be fun."

"Can I get a shot at taking her up, dad?"

"Sure, with me beside you. Are you rated multi-engine, Son?"

"Well, yeah…but mine are jet, not piston." Bill mused.

"Just kidding son. I don't think you'll have a problem with her once you get used to the power difference. I think it'll be fun going up with you." Harry said.

Before the sun went down Generals Reynolds and Hancock had paid their last respects to Jim with a salute down the runway. Several cars took them to the state airport where they caught their flights back to Barksdale and Flagstaff. George stayed behind for a day at Harry's place. He would catch a flight back to Shreveport on Monday.

Harry offered to fly him back in the Electra. George was surprised.

"Would you really do that for me, Harry?"

"Yes, I would George. It would be my honor. We can leave first thing in the morning. You'll be home by supper time."

"That would be great. Thanks, Harry."

As the sun came up over the eastern US, Harry, George, and Bill were already up prepping *Ginny for* a long day in the air. Harry asked George to sit in the right seat while Billie watched the goings-on from behind. George was now near 90, and never having sat up front, Harry and Bill could see George's chest swell with the excitement of 'being up front.'

Ellie had prepared a cooler of lunches and drinks for them, and waved goodbye as they lifted off. A chill came over her watching the *Ginny's Gin* disappear into the western darkness, the red taillight fading quickly. She hoped it was just the chill of the early morning air that caused the shiver.

The three men said little on the flight, all of them watching the sun come up behind them, casting long shadows on the short hills before reaching the Appalachian Mountains.

George looked down at the spreading countryside, something foreign to him compared with view he never saw from 35,000ft inside the B-52.

"Wow!" he exclaimed. "Did I really miss this much of America all those years Jim and I were up there?" he pointed up to the heavens.

"Different, huh George?" Harry asked.

"I never realized how beautiful our country is. The Air Force doesn't show you this." He turned in his seat to look at Billie. "You don't see this either, do you?"

"No, George, I don't. It is beautiful." The two of them in awe of what lie below them, so dramatically different than what they see acting as a line of defense for our country.

"You don't want to sell this plane, dad. I'm going to need it to show my kids what America looks like. Picture books and photographs just don't cut it."

Harry smiled inside himself at what he was doing for a good friend, and his son.

It was time to get out and stretch. George suggested they might want to do more than stretch. They landed at the Charleston South Carolina Joint Air Base and were directed to a parking area on the far end of the runway. A fuel truck topped off the tanks while the men hit the rest rooms. Bill made the suggestion to explore the terminal and find out what was available to them, something different than the sandwiches Ellie had prepared.

"Ok. We can do that." Harry agreed.

Billie walked down the first hallway and found a pizza shop. "Hey, this looks good."

"Alright if that's what you want." Harry and George followed.

One large pizza and three beers held them over for an hour. Now it was time to get back to the plane. The grounds manager told Harry how happy he was to see such a beautiful classic grace his airport. Harry thanked him and made the excuse to leave.

"Got another 600 miles to Shreveport. Hope to make it tonight. Thanks for your hospitality. See you again sometime."

Airborne again by 1400, George had decided to sit in the back and let Bill study the array of newfangled instruments staring at him.

"Oh," Bill said, with surprise. "I know what all these are, dad. This is first generation stuff. My ride has 6th generation. But these are great for the Electra. You're way ahead of other small aircraft."

"That's what Jim said. He spent enough for this stuff. I've been all over the manuals and I think I've got a hold of them all. You shouldn't have a problem, at all, son. Take the wheel."

"Are you sure?" Bill asked.

Harry looked at his son and made the comment,

"If I can't trust a relic from 1935 in the hands of a B-2 bomber pilot, I've got to get out and walk."

Harry turned around to get George's reaction.

"What do think, George? Can I trust him with the controls?"

George didn't move. Harry tied to wake him, but quickly realized that George was no longer with them.

Bill looked at his father. "What's wrong, dad?"

The blankness on Harry's face told the story.

"George is gone, Bill. I'll take the wheel, son. Would you cover him, please?"

Bill covered George with a blanket and turned back, blessing himself, as if to say a silent prayer for George.

"Do we go on to Shreveport?"

"Yeah. His family is buried there. Can you call Shreveport and let them know we coming in with a corpse? We will be requesting an ambulance."

"Is this a case of his wings being done, dad?"

"Yeah, I think so, son. I am surprised his daughter, Ollie, hasn't shown up. She said she would be here to bring her father home."

"Ollie?' Bill asked.

"Oh, you don't know about Ollie. She was your father's first love, many years ago. That was before you were born."

"And she was George's daughter?"

"Yep."

"Do you want to tell me the story?"

Harry looked at his son with indecision. Then said,

"Sure. We have time." Harry told Billie everything, even about the wings and the visitations of Ollie and his grandfather. "Your grandmother, Liz and Jim, came to me, too. "

"So now you think Ollie is going to come and see you?"

"Oh, she'll come. I just don't know where. It could be up here. I don't know."

"Just then, a wisp of smoke rose up from the dash-board."

Billie jumped and yelled at his father, "What's that's dad? Do we have a fire?"

"No, son. We do not have a fire. Come out, Ollie."

Ollie appeared on the windshield in front of Harry.

"I told you I would be back to get my father, Harry."

"So, I guess his wings are ready for delivery, Ollie?"

"Yes. You can deliver his body to Shreveport," Ollie told him.

"Have you been making the rounds, Ollie?"

Billie is dumb founded. He doesn't see anything, but he hears his father talking to the windshield.

"Why don't you introduce yourself to my son, Ollie?"

"Do you think he'll believe, Harry?"

"In time, Ollie. He wasn't reared with the knowledge of the wing stories. I didn't have a reason to bring it up."

"Then I'll wait. He's got enough to think about right now. Do you want a push, Harry? I can help you get there a little sooner."

"A tail wind, Ollie? Sure, go head."

"Is this all for real, dad?" Billie asked.

"I'm afraid so, Bill. Don't worry about it now. I'll explain it all to you when we get back home."

"Good deal, Harry," Ollie said.   'I'll see you in Shreveport."

CHAPTER 28

At Wings End

Harry brought the Electra down at Barksdale Air Force Base with a greeting of an honor guard and an ambulance. He radioed ahead to have the tower notify the General that an airman was coming home.

Maj. General Richard Samples was now base commander following the retirement of Maj. General Harold Reynolds. Military tough, he was a stickler for following procedure and the Air Force way. His physique and mind set belong in the Army, a Task Force, a special weapons unit, or possibly a Navy SEAL. But he was also a very proud individual who loved the military and the rules, regulations, and traditions. He stood alongside the honor guard and the ambulance watching the Lockheed come in, eventually taxiing to its place near the terminal.

The ambulance attendants removed George's body with a reverence befitting a king. Harry told the coroner, who was there when he landed, George died at approximately 1500 hrs., this day. The coroner asked,

"How did he seem, up there?"

"He was good," Harry told him. "We left a pizza shop, in the terminal, about two hours before the flight. Every-body was good, ready to get back in the air. George gave Bill the right seat and he went out back to lie down."

"It was pretty quiet up there, in the plane." Harry was trying to relay everyone's mood just before George died. Billie and I were talking low, softly, careful not to wake George. About an hour into the flight, Bill said something I found to be funny, and I laughed. I fully expected George to laugh knowing his sense of humor. But George did not laugh. In fact, he didn't move. I reached over and touched his hand…cold. I turned to Billie and said, ''George is gone." Billie turned to see I was right and covered the body with a blanket. Then I radioed in and informed the tower."

"Ok, that's all I need. I'll have autopsy results tomorrow morning. I'll check with you later."

The General approached, with the honor guard, and followed the ambulance to the hospital. With Vicky, George's wife, and Olivia, his daughter, both having predeceased him, there were no relatives to notify of his passing.

George Gamer was 93 years old and lived a good life. The friends he made as an airman, and as a respected enthusiast of the B-52, standing on the sideline, will have the honor of sending him off with all the respect due a retired Airman. The following Tuesday, George was cremated, and his ashes scattered over the Mississippi tributary area he called home. There was no plot upon which to put a stone. He and Vicky did not want to take up space in the Veterans Cemetery. He told the church,

"Find a couple of 2 X 4s and make a cross. Get a big rock and scribble our names on it. Put them together, and there's the Gamer cemetery."

George told Jim that act of rebellion cost him $2000, the cost of a headstone. He figured he was even with the government. But Harry and Bill insisted on a stone to mark their friend's resting place. If nothing else, it told people George, Victoria, and Olivia Gamer once walked this earth.

Harry and Bill used base housing for the night. They waited for Ollie to make another appearance, but she never came. Harry signed the necessary papers and took possession of the ashes. He and Bill brought back an empty urn after scattering the ashes where George wished. There was no fanfare, no pomposity, just George's wish,

"Let me walk the bayous and back waters of the Delta with my wife and daughter."

Billie woke up at 0700 AM, in the right seat, at 12000ft. Until that time he was a zombie. Harry woke him early to start the day, wanting to get home before sundown. Bill's stomach started growling when he remembered the sandwiches Ellie had packed in the cooler, two days ago. He wasn't sure they would still be good, or at least edible. He looked at Harry, who looked back over the top of his sunglasses.

"Dad?" Bill asked, "Would you take the chance?"

"On what, eating them? You've got good insurance."

"Oh, come on. Do you think these sandwiches are still good?"

"Well, slowly open the lid, and if you don't smell anything foul, take a look at the sandwiches. They must be in baggies?" Harry asked.

"Yeah, looks like." Bill told him.

"Ok. Now, take one out and show it to me."

Bill removed one sandwich and opened the baggie. He stuck his nose down in the bag to sniff when Harry said,

"Wait." Harry stopped him.

"What? What's the matter, dad? Do you smell something?"

"I don't know. Wait a minute. Let me see that." Harry grabbed the sandwich and looked it over. Then bit the sandwich in half." He looked at Bill and gave him a big grin.

"Dad!" he yelled. You knew the sandwich was good, didn't you? Why didn't you tell me? You used to do that to me when I was a kid. Well, you have your half. The rest is mine."

"You can have it, son. I don't want anymore. I'm not a big breakfast eater. If that's coffee your mother packed for us, I'll have mine."

Bill reached down and brought up a can of cold coffee.He showed Harry, who said, "Aw!"

"That's y our mother's coffee. Well, if that's all there is, I'll have one. Crack one open for me, will ya?"

Harry took a sip and thought a minute over the flavor. "I can see why she likes it. That shit is sweet, but I bet it'll keep you awake."

"Wet is wet, I guess." Harry checked his time in the air and had Bill calculate a course to Dayton, Ohio and Wright-Patterson.

"It's half-way home, dad. Are we gonna refuel and keep going?" Bill asked.

"I think so, Bill. We don't need to get your mother worrying."

Wright-Patterson was a fill-up, and an extra hour showing off the Electra to the mechanics and line crews of the other carriers coming in. Harry saw his time was dwindling. He wanted up and, on his way, long before sunset. It was wheels up at 17:00PM and the nose pointed North-East.

"Another three hours, son, and we can have seafood for supper."

"That would sure be a lot better than three-day-old sandwiches." Bill added.

Harry pulled out a cigarette and sat back to cruise and watch the sun slowly sink below the horizon. The sky screamed at them a bright glowing red and yellow. The sky blue bleach-washed into the mix.

Bill watched the light reflected on the lakes and ponds as they crossed the eastern quarter of this country.

"It all looks so mesmerizing, dad. You have to pay attention and separate the real from the hypnotically un-real." He let out a breath and confessed, "but I can't wait to get home."

"Me, too, son. Me, too." The rest of the trip was quiet. Both men were tired of the flight, the thrumming of the engines, the bumpy runways, and not having the relaxing comfort of a steady home and a home cooked meal. But today, they both savored some good seafood.

Harry had plotted a course over Scranton, headed for Albany. As they crossed the NY line into Massachusetts Bill called Ellie to give her their location, and the approximate time they would be touching down at T.F. Green.

"Hello," Ellie answered.

"Hi, mom. It's Bill. Dad and I just crossed the NY line into Massachusetts and should be landing at T.F. Green in about an hour. Can you pick us up?"

"You're damn right!" Ellie hung up the phone and rushed to clean up for her husband. She had thirty minute to get to the airport. The keys to the convertible were ready and available. She grabbed them and ran out the door. The Mustang convertible had a standard shift, but Harry had taught her how to drive it and how to handle the extra horsepower. Ellie couldn't always avoid squealing the tires, but sometimes she enjoyed the sound. Only the just-barely-over-60 crowd in the neighborhood loved it.

With the top down she was able to watch for a streak of silver passing over, headed for the airport. As she made the gate onto the field, she saw the Electra make its descent onto the runway. Ellie drove to the hangar and waited. She could hear the blip-blip-blip of the radial engines as it came closer to her. *Ginny's Gin* stopped in front of the hangar and Ellie watched her two weary men escape the airborne cocoon for terra-firma. Bill got out and gave his mother a hug and a kiss. He turned to watch his father bend down to kiss the earth.

"You still do that, dad?" Bill asked.

"Tradition, son. Tradition."

Rushing up to meet her husband she gave him a big kiss disguised a s a hug.

"Miss me?" he asked.

"You betcha," she responded. "Staying home, a while?" she asked.

"You betcha," he answered. Ellie handed the keys to Billie to dive home. Harry told him,

"Just keep it under a hundred."

"Will do." Billie got behind the wheel and saw a third pedal. "Dad?" He asked. "What is this other pedal for?"

"What 'other' pedal, son?"

"The one on the outside of the brake?"

Harry and Ellie looked at one another and laughed.

"I never did teach you how to drive a stick, did I?"

"A stick?"

"A standard transmission. They were very popular when I was your age. I guess I'll have to drive home. Ellie, would you mind sitting in the back while this young man pays attention to the choreography of the hands and feet?"

"I would be happy to, professor." Ellie jumped in the back. Billie took the right seat, and Harry began with lesson number one of driving a standard Boss Mustang 302 SHO. Harry pulled out of the parking spot and Bill's first words were, "Holy Shit!"

The rest of the ride was quiet, but tense. Harry tried to play Steve McQueen, from the movie *Bullet,* while Billie watched the speedometer actually hit the 100. Harry watched his son trying to figure out how this car could go this fast and not get off the ground. Harry asked, "Is it anything like your B-2, Billie?"

"No, dad, not quite." Billie only let go of the dashboard when his father stopped in the parking lot of his favorite seafood restaurant. He watched his mother and father climb out the Mustang and walk toward the restaurant.

"Are you coming? I thought you wanted seafood." Harry asked.

"I'm going back to Maine and the B-2," Bill told them

Ellie urged him, "Come and have something to eat first."

Billie ran to the back of the car and heaved up what little he had in his stomach from the flight.

"Are you okay, Bill?" his father asked.

"Yeah. I'm okay. I dropped my watch." He then joined his mother and father inside for his last meal with them before driving back to Maine.

CHAPTER 29

Feather In A Cup

The restaurant was near capacity, but any restaurant along the Rhode Island coast was going to fill up quickly. The threesome was led to a booth on the ocean side. A breakwater of rock and jersey barriers kept the ocean from taking away the establishment. One hundred feet of sand and shell bits gave the public something to walk on.

Harry and Ellie ordered some refreshment while Billie tried to tell himself he was hungry. The menu had something he knew he could keep down, the clam chowder, and plenty of crackers.

No one was sitting behind them, but Harry felt sure he felt someone tap him on the shoulder. Ellie watched his face and his posture stiffen. Harry looked at her and she knew what was happening. It was Ollie. Ellie stared at the picture window and could see Ollie looking back at her.

Billie got up to go to the men's room. That gave Ollie a chance to speak to the two of them. Whispering, Harry asked, "On the job, Ollie?"

She nodded yes.

Harry asked, "How's George?"

"He's good, Harry. Thank you for bringing him home."

"He was a friend, Ollie." Harry told her, afraid to ask her one question.

Ellie spoke up. Are you picking someone up, Ollie, tonight?"

Ollie nodded again.

Ellie told her, "No, Ollie, not tonight."

Harry heard the assertive, determined words Ellie aimed at Ollie. Who had the power here? Can you argue with an angel and win? There was only one power that would make the final decision, the Boss, and Ollie had to be following orders.

Billie returned as the waitress brought out the appetizers. "What's wrong, guys…mom, dad? What do you see out the window, dad?"

"An old relic, son," he whispered…"an old relic."

Billie could see there was no old relic out the window. And then he saw a vision reflecting back at him. With some uncertainty he asked his mother,

"What am I looking at, mom? There's a face on the window, but I'm not sure it's really there."

Two highly educated men, who, with complete discernment, pilot multi-million dollar aircraft carrying doomsday in their bellies. On a split second's notice, they were capable of making decisions that would slay or save a person's life. Now they were faced with an entity that no longer belonged to this world. Was Ollie interfering in the Harry's and Billie's lives? It didn't seem to them she had the power to do so. But, there she presented herself.

Ellie began telling her son the words his grandfather used to say about leaving this earth…"Not until my wings were done." She told him how those who believe in angels will sometime experience visits from the angels of recently deceased relatives. Those angels hang around, refuse to leave, until their wings are done.

"Ollie is one of those angels, Billie. She was also your father's first love, and she was George Gamer's daughter."

"But how does that impact my grandfather?"

"We don't know, yet. But Ollie has been around several times recently to collect her mother and her father. She was here when your grandmother left us, and Jim. But she's not taking anyone now, not without a fight from me."

Ollie heard the words her friend was telling her son but did not speak to Billie. Harry spoke to Ollie and asked,

"Who is it now, Ollie?"

She would not give him an answer, but then said,

"I can't tell you who, Harry, only that it won't be long."

"Can we enjoy our dinner now, Ollie?" and she left.

"Alright, Ollie's gone. Let's eat before the night passes away again."

Several hours passed with talk about the angels and how they have interacted with Harry's family down through the years.

"Why our family, dad, mom?"

"I don't know, son. No one has ever tried to figure it out.

As the meal ended and Harry got ready to pay the bill, he noticed a feather in the teacup Ellie used with her tea.

His mind going through the sadness of funerals, he picked up the feather and put it in his pocket. Quietly he turned toward the window and told Ollie,

"It's not going to happen, Ollie. I'll fight you till hell freezes over."

CHAPTER 30

History's Connection

Two weeks after returning from Louisiana, Olivia Johnson called saying her husband had passed. The obituary listed Sam as one of the last remaining WWII veterans in the country. He spent 8 months in England before being shipped out to the Pacific theater, fighting side by side with the So. Koreans. Oliver Ackworth had enlisted in 1938, and at 26, fought in a war half way around the world.

Harry was heartbroken. He really wanted to explore the album, ask questions and get answers for his own ancestry. Ellie called Olivia to extend the family's condolences. She asked if Olivia would like some company. Olivia said she would be more than happy to have them come by.

The West Cranston facility was not far from Harry's home. Harry and Ellie had no problem finding the place. Olivia watched from her second floor balcony, as they came up the drive.

Billie was home that weekend and asked Olivia if he could tag along.

"Absolutely, son. Come learn of your grandfather and the history he shared with my Sam."

After condolences were passed between the grievers Ellie helped Olivia bring out a tray of snacks and a large pitcher of iced tea. The men explored the photos and newspaper articles Sam had saved. Many of them faded and delicate to being difficult to read. It was very warm outside and many of the retired tenants were enjoying the pool. Olivia enjoyed entertaining her guests with old stories and snacks, also the air-conditioning.

"Mrs. Johnson, I do hope your husband was accurate about some of this."

"Sonny, if there is one thing my Sam was, it was accurate. Throwing a knife, shooting a gun, pistol or rifle, Sam was very good in all disciplines. Why do you ask?"

"I'm confused. It's the names, and one last name in particular, Johnson."

"That could be. My Sam was a Johnson, and I took his name."

"Yes," Billie pointed out, "and my grandfather, Oliver. He married an Alice Johnson. Was there a connection between my grandmother and your husband?"

"Not that Sam ever mentioned to me. He did say he thought he had a sister. He remembers playing with a little girl when he was a growing up. His father left when Sam was young, and he and his mother went to live in another city. His sister went to another relative, or at least that's what Sam was told. He tried looking for her but never found her."

"That memory grew old, and Sam never thought Oliver's wife could be his sister. They only chummed around a little while they were all in Korea. Last names didn't matter, then. Alice was an Army nurse got pregnant when Oliver took leave. She never told him, and he was killed chasing a Mig. She returned to the states, had Donald, and then died before he graduated elementary school."

"He grew up as the ward of a Catholic home for kids in Boston. And that's as far as that part of your history goes."

"Sam found a small piece about a B-29 and a bombardier that almost fell out the plane. He found it interesting because the last name was Ackworth, and that was Oliver's last name, his friend from Korea. He dug not it and found that Ackworth was Oliver's kid. Sam couldn't believe the luck of coming across something like that, after so many years have gone by."

Harry said, "That was my father." Harry turned to Ellie and told her his father never said he was a ward of the church. My mother never knew, and that's why I never met my grandparents. They had already passed. There was no one to meet."

"Ollie, dad. Why does she come around our family?"

Ellie thought, "Let's look at the names, the last names, particularly Johnson."

"Great grandfather Oliver marries Alice Johnson. Coincidentally, Oliver has a mechanic in Korea named Sam Johnson whose younger sister goes missing, or at least they are separated, at a young age. He can't find her, but an Alice Johnson shows up as an Army nurse in Korea. She gets pregnant by OIiver and has the child in Boston. No one makes a connection between Sam and Alice, that they were brother and sister.

"But why does Ollie get involved?" Let's look at George and Vicky's last names."

"George as a Gamer, Victoria was…a Johnson!" Every-one looks at one another and bells goes off."

Olivia Johnson is listening and smiling at the conclusions every-one is drawing.

"You mentioned Ollie and why does she continue to come around. I'm guessing you are referring to Victoria's daughter, Olivia. Vicky was my Sam's second sister. Sam's mother had another child after they moved out of the city. That was Victoria. They kept in touch over the years but lost contact as George dragged the family around following the bombers, base to base. So, Ollie, as you call her, is following the Johnson kin and handing them their wings as they become ready."

Harry looked at Olivia and realized she was the next one whose wings are ready. She was to be the next to go. Olivia smiled at him, recognizing he knew the answer to the family puzzle. Ellie caught the interaction cautioning Bill to stop trying to figure it out.

"I'll tell you later," she told him. e grw upHe

Olivia went into her bedroom and brought out a small sheaf of papers along with the album. Inside was a hand written note from her husband. It read,

> *"This synopsis was drawn up to add clarity and completeness to the articles and photographs here in.*
>
> *Sam also wrote, "To seek information on a product you have to use that product. I found that which I thought to be seeking, to be less than imagined in the container."*
>
> *Thank you, Jim, Harry, and William for your dedication and patriotism to your country. It shall not go unnoticed."*

Thank You,
Lt. Sam Johnson
US Air Force
Suwon Air Base
Rep. So. Korea

Olivia and her guests spent an entire afternoon going through Sam's album. They laughed a little at the ridiculousness of men posing for photos. They cried reading of the destruction throughout South Korea and the children wantonly slaughtered by the North Koreans. Harry and Bill took special interest in the articles on the F-86 and the exploits of the American pilots, especially one, Cpt. Oliver Ackworth, an Ace. The afternoon was history revisited by Olivia and a new history uncovered for Harry and Bill.

Harry said, "My father would have liked to a have known his father."

"We now know why he didn't get to."

"Alice was pregnant when your grandfather was shot down. And no one knew until it was time for the baby to be born."

"All the pieces fit, Olivia. Thank you for giving the opportunity to answer the questions that fill in the missing pieces. My grandfather was an Ace…like you, dad. You were an Ace in Iran."

"Yeah. But it's not being an Ace that's important, it's coming home. Speaking of home. We have to let this fine lady go to supper with her friends. We've kept her long enough."

"Oh," Olivia said, "You can join me for supper, if you'd like to. It's allowed. The meals are quite good. I think you'll like it. Tonight's it's meat loaf with gravy."

Harry and Ellie looked at Bill waiting for an answer.

"Sure, why not. Can't hurt." Bill said.

Olivia checked with the dining room master and three extra plates were set at Olivia's table.

"Smells good," Harry said. Bill agreed, but Ellie thought there might be something missing, and she could smell it.

Bill was the first to recognize the difference between Ellie's meatloaf and what the Home was serving its tenants. Harry and Ellie looked at one another and both reached for the saltshaker. There wasn't one on the table.

"No salt, Olivia?" he asked.

"Oh, no. Not here. We are not allowed to have salt. It raises your blook pressure, you know. The pepper is quite good at seasoning the food. It's different. Try it."

Harry grabbed the pepper and liberally sprinkled some on his meatloaf. After trying the meat, he accepted it as 'passable.'

Bill's quiet whisper was, "Deadly!"

Ellie heard the comment and laughed, watching her husband shake his head. He wondered how the home can legally serve that food to the residents.

Harry, Ellie, and Billie hung on until desert came by and then made an excuse to leave. Ellie told Olivia,

"We are terribly sorry, Oliva, but we do have to go. We should have been more mindful of the time. Bill has to get back to the base. It has been a distinct pleasure spending the afternoon with you and discovering Harry's history and his long lost grandfather. Thank you so much for your hospitality."

"Perhaps we can do it again, sometime?" Oliva asked.

"But of course," Harry told her. Olivia was 92 years and failing rapidly since Sam passed. He turned to Ellie and whispered,

"I think her wings may be ready shortly."

"I think I heard you say my wings are ready. Oh, good. I'm tired of all the rigmarole of being human...and my Sam will be waiting for me. Maybe tonight," Olivia thought.

Harry and Ellie were surprised to hear Olivia speak of her wings, that she even knew they were ready. Ellie looked at Harry, "If you ever find out my wings are ready, please do not tell me. It would upset the rest of my life. I will wait till the end, whether I'm ready for them or not."

"I'll hold on to them for you, dear, but only until my wings are done."

The End

THE AUTHOR

Not as flamboyant as the script above would indicate.

Born in 1947, a Baby Boomer, of the X-TRA large size. I did walk to school in the middle of Winter, uphill both ways. My brothers and sisters and I were often tasked with walking to the village grocery to pick up a few things for mom or a pack of cigarettes for dad.

Siblings, I once had 8, but time and disease has reduced that to 7. Mom and dad are both gone, now, but we children still relish the time we spend together. I dabbled in music, trying to learn to play the trumpet, the piano and to write barbershop harmony. I have been singing barbershop a Capella harmony for almost 27 years and once had my own quartet, *Stateline*. Our greatest achievement was Novice Quartet Champion for 2007.

I enjoy my writing and I enjoy people telling me they enjoy my writing. Those kinds of compliments will keep me writing.

REL